The Katrina Protocol

(A Club Van Helsing ᵗᵐ Adventure)

also by Jean-Marc & Randy Lofficier

from Black Coat Press:

Edgar Allan Poe on Mars
Despair (*screenplay adapted from Marc Agapit*)
Robonocchio
Royal Flush (*original screenplay*)

anthologies
Tales of the Shadowmen:
1. The Modern Babylon - 2. Gentlemen of the Night
3. Danse Macabre - 4. Lords of Terror

translations
Arsène Lupin vs. Sherlock Holmes: The Hollow Needle
Arsène Lupin vs. Sherlock Holmes: The Blonde Phantom
(*adapted from Maurice Leblanc*)
Doc Ardan: City of Gold and Lepers
(*adapted from Guy d'Armen*)
Doctor Omega (*adapted from Arnould Galopin*)
The Phantom of the Opera (*adapted from Gaston Leroux*)

non-fiction
Shadowmen: Heroes and Villains of French Pulp Fiction
Shadowmen 2: Heroes and Villains of French Comics
Over Here: An American Expat in the South of France

from iUniverse:
The Doctor Who Programme Guide
The Nth Doctor - Into the Twilight Zone

The Katrina Protocol
(*A Club Van Helsing* ™ *Adventure*)

by
Jean-Marc Lofficier
adapted by
Randy Lofficier

CVH ™

A Black Coat Press Book

Thanks to David McDonnell for proofreading the typescript.

Visit our website at www.blackcoatpress.com

To Mike Mitchell,
who was there at the beginning,
Xavier Mauméjean and Guillaume Lebeau,
for providing the inspiration,
and David McDonnell,
Keeper of the Faith.

Contents

Foreword

Dear Hunters

When I was eight, I was certain of at least one thing: Count Zaroff would never have killed Bambi's mother.

I reached that staggering conclusion late one Sunday night after my parents had watched *The Most Dangerous Game* on TV. I wasn't allowed to stay up and watch with them because the next day was a school day, but no one could stop me from listening to the soundtrack that filtered through the wall into the room where I slept. That's how I had heard Zaroff with his bizarre accent offer his guests a glass of champagne—followed by a manhunt, to spice up his otherwise monotonous life. That Russian aristocrat might have been lacking in ethics, but he had style, and class, just like another character I also loved, Kraven the Hunter, standing tall and proud in his lion-mane jacket. Zaroff hunted castaways in the dank jungles of his far-away island of Baranka; Kraven hunted the amazing Spider-Man in the concrete jungles of New York. Both loved the thrill of the hunt, its risks and challenges—and behaved according to a certain code of honor which forbade specific actions.

Kraven would never have killed Babar's mother either, I thought, as I finally fell asleep that night.

Many years have gone by, and the magic of Late Night TV has been replaced by videos, then DVDs and films on demand downloadable from the Internet, but I never forgot that crystal-clear insight I had one night before falling asleep. I have since paid homage to the exiled Cossack General created by Richard Connell and the obsessive-compulsive big game hunter created by Stan Lee and Steve Ditko in various works of my own, including my series of novels *The League of Heroes*.[1] Then, one day, Jean-Marc Lofficier offered to publish its first volume in America. I was already familiar with Jean-Marc's (and his wife Randy's) superb editorial and translating work, so I enthusiastically agreed. Working with JM, I came to realize that he, too, had style and class, even without slick, combed back hair or skin-tight leopard print pants.

Two years ago, I created the *Club Van Helsing* imprint with Guillaume Lebeau for French publisher Baleine. Guillaume is another veteran of Late Night TV horror shows; one can tell right away from the near-maniacal gleam which appears in his eyes when one starts discussing how many ways there are to kill a vampire or how many monsters Universal Pictures brought to the screen. We began assembling a team of talented writers according to the mandate we set up: one book, one monster, one hunter, one battle. For reasons I'm afraid to guess, Jean-Marc, when solicited, chose to tackle the theme of zombies, against the background of Hurricane Katrina.

I confess to a certain fondness for the novel he eventually wrote and which is entitled *Crépuscule Vaudou—Voodoo Twilight*—in the original French. First, because it's a captivating tale, with lots of action, and yet quiet moments of erudition and political reflection. It

---

[1] Available in a Black Coat Press edition.

is also a serious novel that manages not to take itself too seriously. And, above all, because under his pen, my co-creation, Hugo Van Helsing, acquired the same style and class as the two dear hunters of my youth.

To you, reader, who have just opened this book, I say: abandon all hope of going to sleep early. Make yourself comfortable in your favorite armchair, or against the pillows, and too bad if tomorrow is a schoolday—or a workday. The game is afoot. The hunt can begin!

Xavier Mauméjean

The Katrina Protocol

Tuesday, August 23, 2005

LONG LIVE LORD ZARYAN!

Mandy had just decided to dump her boy friend Tom when the first bullet tore the left side off of her face.

"Long live Lord Zaryan!" shouted the killer, enthusiastically.

A bloody flower spread its petals in the afternoon sun while from all around, screams of horror erupted.

Frank Clayton—the killer—next targeted an older man wearing a leather jacket over a blue denim shirt. He had been writing in a spiral notebook and when the first shot rang out, had jumped to his feet with surprising speed for someone his age. The bullet from Frank's 9mm semi-automatic Glock 19 hit the man twice in the chest. The victim crumpled to the ground, pulling his chair down with him.

The other patrons sitting on the outside terrace of the Starbucks café located at the intersection of St. Charles and Napoleon Avenue in New Orleans' superb garden district really had only two choices: run into the street, or seek refuge inside the coffee house.

Those who chose to run were, one by one, methodically mowed down by Frank with his semi-automatic Walther P22.

"Long live Lord Zaryan!" repeated the killer every time a victim fell to the ground, dead or soon to be dead.

After he had eliminated all of the *possessed*—the enemies of Lord Zaryan who had fled from his just wrath and were in thrall to the vile Necromancers of the Thirteenth Circle—Frank turned towards the Starbucks entrance.

"Long live Lord Zaryan!" he said again, as he stepped inside the coffee shop. He wanted them to understand that he wasn't crazy. Yes, it was a dirty job, but someone had to do it, and Lord Zaryan had chosen *him* to execute this sacred mission.

A mother who was shielding her eight-year-old daughter with her own body was his next victim.

Frank stopped to laugh at his own joke. *To execute this sacred mission. Execute! Ha! Ha!* He also had to recharge his Glock.

He then shot a gay couple and a medical student, who had chosen to pay for her school tuition by putting on the Starbucks uniform and serving coffee part-time to idle New Orleans residents from Tuesdays to Fridays.

"Long live Lord Zar..." Frank started to say once again, when suddenly his sense of elation turned to searing pain. More specifically, pain emanating from his right leg.

He looked down and saw a large spot of blood already spreading across his slacks, just above his right thigh.

Half-hidden behind an overturned table, Helen, a 35-year-old teacher who had been waiting for a transfer to Alabama where her family lived, had just shot Frank with her Smith & Wesson Model 10. She fired again.

This time, the 19-year-old, hit directly in the chest, fell.

"Long live..." gurgled Frank as his mouth filled with his own blood. Could Lord Zaryan, his God, abandon him thus? Forsake him so completely? Would the vile Necromancers of the Thirteenth Circle—for he had no doubt that the woman who had just shot him was an emanation of Vrek himself—triumph so unjustly?

At last, a dim light illuminated his clouded mind. He had finally remembered that Lord Zaryan, Vrek and the Necromancers of the Thirteenth Circle were nothing more than characters from the latest PlayStation game, *Armageddon 4*.

"Smoking," he whispered.

Then he died.

The police eventually arrived, all sirens blaring. The SWATs, wearing their bulletproof vests, tumbled out of their blue vans like a crowd of ants rushing towards a picnic, ready to shoot on sight. But it was all over and there was nothing for them to do other than start collecting the names of the victims—and notify their families.

Overlooking Port-au-Prince, the somewhat faded yet still attractive neighborhood of Pétionville was the residence of choice for those Haitians who sought to escape the summer's merciless heat.

The rented Land Rover stopped in front of a magnificent villa dating from the mid-19th century, erected on a spectacular spot on the road to Fermathe.

The driver mopped his sweat-drenched forehead. The temperature in the sun was at least 110 degrees. He honked three times, as he had been instructed to do. The old wrought iron gates swung open slowly, jerkily, almost as if a mysterious unseen force was still trying to deny the caller entry.

Inside the villa, the temperature was still hot, but bearable. The visitor stopped for a minute to admire the impregnable view across the bay of Port-au-Prince through the picture windows.

"I am glad to make your acquaintance, Mister Corona," said the owner of the house, speaking in English with a heavy Haitian accent. He was a mulatto, tall and powerful-looking. His head was round and his shiny, black hair, strangely slick, was combed back from his domed forehead. He wore freshly ironed, lightweight, white clothes.

"*Moi aussi*, Monsieur Legendre," said his visitor in impeccable Metropolitan French.

"You have brought... what we discussed?" asked Legendre, pointing towards his guest's leather briefcase. Then, noticing that it was tied to the man's wrist by a discreet metal chain, he added, "That is... unadvisable. In Haiti, we tell parents to write their children's names on the soles of their feet, because sometimes, they lose their heads."

This reference to the *Rats-à-kaka*, armed gangs connected to the Aristide clan who still spread murder and terror in the city, did not appear to impress the visitor.

With quick and efficient gestures, Corona put the briefcase on the table, worked its combination lock and opened it. Inside was a primitive, African-style dagger with a strangely carved ebony handle and an ivory blade. The pommel of the handle resembled a double-axe and was decorated with silver inlays.

"Ah, the Dagger of Hevioso," whispered Legendre, taking the knife and handling it with the respect one generally reserves for precious religious icons. "My grandfather would be proud to see it once again in the hands of its legitimate owner."

"Legitimate isn't quite the way I would put it," said Carlo Corona with a note of irony. "If I believe our archives, your grandfather, the aptly-named 'Murder' Legendre, slaughtered an entire village to get his hands on this dagger." Then, seeing the dark cloud that had come over his host's face, he hurried to add: "But I'm not here to judge him—or you. Our terms are quite straightforward, Monsieur Legendre. If you do exactly what BlackSpear asks of you, you may keep this dagger—and the other three talismans. That is, if you can get your 'legitimate' hands on them."

"Then you will not be disappointed, Mister Corona. Tell the ones who've sent you that, very soon, New Orleans shall be *breathless in silk, lying in the bay of Death.*"

"I beg your pardon?"

"It's from a poem by Magloire-Saint-Aude.[2] One of our greatest poets. *Au revoir*, Mister Corona."

That same night, much farther to the south and east of Port-au-Prince, in the Bahamas, a tropical depression began to form...

---

[2] Clément Magloire-Sainte-Aude (1912-1971), writer and poet, author of *Dialogue de mes lampes* [Dialogue of my Lamps] and *Tabou* [Taboo] (both 1941). Legendre is quoting the poem *Poison*, included in the former collection.

15

Thursday, August 25

IN MY BUSINESS, EVERY DEATH IS SUSPECT.

From the Diaries of Hugo Van Helsing

I hadn't set foot in New Orleans for 20 years and yet, I had butterflies in my stomach, just as if it had been yesterday. I felt wretched and miserable and I bet it must have shown on my face, considering the looks I was getting from the other travelers.

The airport seemed larger, roomier than I remembered it to be. Everything was attractive, new and sparkling.

I didn't like it.

I much preferred the old airport, when it was called Moisant. The city had renamed it "Louis Armstrong" in 2001 to celebrate the 100-year anniversary of the birth of the man who was arguably its greatest son. Don't get me wrong, I love Armstrong, but I would have been much happier if they hadn't forever linked his name to this modern monstrosity. It was a sinister airport, full of harassed people who trod grudgingly beneath its concrete arches without ever taking notice of each other. It was an already defiled carcass that served as a temple for the tired anonymity that passed for convenience in today's transportation industry.

Next to me, my attorney and trusted ally, Zigor Side, was patiently waiting for our luggage to arrive. Zigor (his first name comes from his Basque ancestors and appropriately means "punishment") looked like the aging hippie he was, somewhat unkempt, in need of a good night's sleep, a cigarette, a cup of coffee and a drink—not necessarily in that order. At least he was in total harmony with our miserable surroundings. Knowing his touching faith in '70s psychobabble, I was certain that, had he been able to read my thoughts, he would have said that my "aura" was full of "negativity."

Wrong!

The best proof was that I had sworn to never again set foot in New Orleans—and yet, here I was.

Zigor believed that good fortune smiled on the bold. He believed in all kinds of rubbish. As far as I was concerned, there were only two kinds of bold: the rich and the dead. The trick was to not end up in the latter category.

I could have stayed in New Orleans and studied with my uncle Ohisver, who wanted nothing more than to groom me to take over the family business, as it were. I could have made money, lots of money probably. And he would have been so proud to have his worthy nephew follow in his footsteps... Hugo Van Helsing, a true Van Helsing to the core...

But fate spins her web without taking into account the mortal wishes of uncles and nephews. Uncle Ohisver was dead, and I was back in New Orleans.

American Airlines was true to its word and our luggage arrived without a glitch. On the curb outside I watched Zigor. Out of respect for my presumed sorrow, no doubt, he remained silent. He had guessed that I wasn't quite ready yet to tackle the consequences of my uncle's death... to deal with the enormity of the tragedy...

The cab driver put the suitcases in the trunk and asked for our destination. A sudden flash of inspiration made me tell him to drop us at the corner of Canal and St. Charles, right in the middle of downtown, just outside the *Vieux Carré*, the French Quarter.

Zigor was surprised. His respect for my privacy hadn't suppressed his professional curiosity. It was quite understandable really. One didn't become one of the country's leading trial lawyers, a member of three State Bars, without being afflicted with a bottomless case of curiosity.

"Where are we going?" he asked.

"Geographically or philosophically?" I replied dryly.

"Aw, c'mon, Professor, don't play games with me. You know what I mean. Why aren't we going to Saint-Amadou?"

"To be honest, I'm not ready to go home yet."

Zigor nodded; although he looked like an oddball, I knew that was just an impression he liked to give. In reality, he was as smart as they come and a whiz at picking up subtle behavior clues, as the many witnesses he had demolished during cross-examination had learned to their surprise. He had already guessed I was hesitant about returning to Saint-Amadou. That was the name of the Van Helsings' ancestral home in New Orleans, built by Ithamar Van Helsing, in 1816. It is a house unlike any other and for any Van Helsing, it really is *the* House, with a capital H.

"If you feel too bummed out," he said, "I can take care of all of your uncle's funeral arrangements. That's why I came."

"No, thanks, that's not really the problem."

How could I explain to him what Uncle Ohisver and the House truly meant to me? My favorite uncle... The place where I had spent all my summer holidays when I was a child... The city where I sowed my youthful wild oats—and there were no wilder oats than mine... It was here that I took my first, tentative steps onto the other side of the Inconstant Shore... It was all that, and more that I felt at that moment. We Van Helsings are not like other people and Uncle Ohisver was a second father to me, probably more important than my own father had been. It was he who had educated me, and I don't mean math, Latin or chemistry—I mean the *other* education... The education specially reserved for Van Helsings.

How could I explain to Zigor Side, who had grown up an orphan in Hell's Kitchen in New York, what it felt like to suddenly lose one's father, teacher and youth all at the same time?

"What is your problem then?" said Zigor.

Now, he was playing at being a therapist. He could be very good at that, too. I knew he wouldn't give me a moment's rest until I satisfied his curiosity. He's like that, Zigor, and that's why I pay him the big bucks.

"Uncle Ohisver kept many secrets," I said. "Dark and powerful secrets..."

Now, he understood, or rather, he thought he understood. In fact, he didn't understand at all, but that alone would be enough to keep him quiet—at least I thought so.

"Do you think there may be some kind of occult motive behind the Massacre?"

Ah-ha!—the criminologist had now come to take the place of the therapist. The game was afoot!

The "Massacre" was where my uncle had died. The media had coined the name: *The Napoleon Avenue Massacre*. They had been all over it during the last 48 hours.

I was astonished they hadn't yet scraped some of the blood off the pavement to sniff it.

A 19-year-old man, Frank Clayton, had killed 14 people, including my uncle Ohisver, who was his second victim. It had been an insane, mindless slaughter, with no apparent motive, and, sadly, it was the kind of tragedy that was happening with disturbing frequency across America.

I was in New York with Zigor and our friends the Lycaons when I had heard the news. We were discussing our plans to prevent the Clock Company from taking over the Misquamacas Trading Company, which owned every Indian burial site in the Dakotas.

My secretary at Bedlam forwarded the call. That was how I learned that my uncle had just been killed by a lunatic. The policewoman at the other end of the line worked for the New Orleans PD and had been assigned to contact the next of kins. Old Zaka had given her my number when she had gone to Saint-Amadou to give him my uncle's blood-stained spiral notebook and personal effects.

I was, she said, the twelfth person on her list. A dreadful job. I didn't envy her.

"Do you think there may be some kind of occult motive behind the Massacre?" Zigor had asked.

I had wondered the same thing myself.

"I don't think so," I answered, however, but didn't volunteer any more details.

The day before I had called Zaka, who was my uncle's servant, all-purpose handyman and friend. He sounded terribly sad and more than a little bit confused, which was quite understandable considering his age and the circumstances. And it had been a very long time since we'd spoken to each other...

I did not tell Zigor that Zaka had asked me to come at once, urgently—without explaining why.

The cab dropped us at the corner of Canal and St. Charles, as instructed.

I started to breathe in the sweet smells of the *Vieux Carré*—the aroma of Cajun cooking blending with the powerful odors of the flowers that decorate the wrought iron balconies.

We crossed Canal and entered the French Quarter, which should really be called the Creole Quarter, as it doesn't really look very much like France. Uncle Ohisver had brought me here many times when I was a child. Until that minute, I hadn't realized how much I'd missed New Orleans.

It was the beginning of the afternoon. The French Quarter was barely awake and only beginning to dream of the night's festivities. I thought I caught a note or two from a trumpet blaring somewhere, or perhaps I was just imagining—no, *remembering* it. In my head, past and present intermingled, images of my youth freely resurfaced to superimpose themselves with what I saw; nights in jazz clubs, playing a trumpet until sunrise, the girls, some easy, others less so, Mardi-Gras of course, with its intoxicating atmosphere of round-the-clock partying...

"Why?" asked Zigor suddenly, tearing me away from my remembrances of things past.

"Why what?"

"Why did you stop talking to your uncle?"

"We had words."

"What kind of words?"

He could be worse than a pitbull with a bone. Sometimes, I wondered if one of his Basque ancestors hadn't served in the Holy Inquisition.

"It's complicated... My uncle wanted me to follow in his footsteps, like my father... You know my family's rather unique vocation... But I was at an age when rebellion comes naturally. The notion of a preordained destiny, a life entirely planned for me, was unbearable. And then, there was that nasty business in Cambridge, at the University... *The Whistling Room*... I refused to acknowledge my own responsibilities and blamed my family for the whole thing. I was angry at my father and at Uncle Ohisver, so I quit. I traveled; I went—you know where. I stayed there for six years. After that, my uncle never forgave me. He refused to speak to me. As far as he was concerned, I was dead to him."

"And yet—what about the Club? It's something you can be proud of. Your father was proud of you. Did you ever try to tell your uncle about it?"

"No. I never found the time. I did write him a letter once, but he never replied. And then, I got busy... You know what our existence is like..."

"It's too bad," he said.

"Yes."

We turned into Bienville, a small street lined with brightly-colored houses that is charming but not particularly memorable. It was hot and muggy—a storm was brewing—but if one stayed in the shade, the walk was not altogether unpleasant.

"It's pretty around here," said Zigor. "Are we there yet?"

"Almost. That's where we're going."

I pointed to a small occult shop, discreet to the point of not even having a painted sign outside it. It was located slightly off the street, set back slightly and sandwiched between two larger houses. There was a small glass window and an entrance hidden behind a dusky red velvet curtain. It was the kind of shop one expects to find in the French Quarter, offering all the easy paraphernalia for the aspiring or amateur occultist: fancy tarot cards sets, crystal balls, amulets, grimoirs, red and black candles, herbs and other less savory ingredients, charms, etc. I had visited shops just like it from Boston to San Francisco.

But we were in New Orleans and, there, even a shop like this one can hold secrets that remain hidden from the average tourist or occasional amateur.

I went in and Zigor followed me.

A young Creole woman in her early twenties stood behind the counter. She was petite and astonishingly beautiful, with eyes black as night and a mop of curly red hair that made her head look as if it was on fire. Some might have thought it came from a bottle; I was sure it didn't.

"Can I help you?" she asked with a spellbinding smile.

Zigor immediately started puffing up like Tex Avery's Wolf when he met Little Red Riding Hood. I realized that if I didn't step in, the girl was going to sell him three-quarters of the store before he knew what hit him.

"We've just received some powder of crushed black lotus," she whispered confidentially, displaying a jar that contained what I could see was ordinary African musk and, in my opinion, not even of the highest grade.

"I'm Professor Hugo Van Helsing," I said, "and I've come to see Marie."

The sharp sound of the glass jar that she had almost dropped onto the counter when she heard my name, reverberated through the store like a cannon shot. Her smile vanished as quickly as had the prospect of a lucrative sale.

"Professor Hugo Van Helsing?"

"Yes. And you are...?"

"Ascension Proudfoot. I'm Oya's latest handmaiden."

"I see. What happened to Patience?"

"Miss Latrelle now practices in Shanghai. She left about five years ago."

"I wish I was a more frequent customer," I said, flashing my brightest smile at her; it was the one most likely to inspire confidence.

She pressed the small button of an electric bell and smiled back.

"As you can see, we've replaced the old brass bell. We're making an effort to move on with the times."

"It mustn't be easy. I know Marie and her aversion to any kind of modernity."

"Well, it did take me three years to persuade her to install this," she admitted, with another endearing smile.

An old Cajun, dressed completely in white, came out of the back room. There was nothing modern about him. He looked like he was a hundred–or more.

"Gaston, would you mind taking these gentlemen to see Oya?" said Ascension.

"*Tout de suite, Mademoiselle*."

Gaston gestured that we should follow him.

We entered the back room. This was where the real items were kept–and sold from behind the counter. The contents of the jars carefully arranged on the shelves had nothing in common with the tourist crap that was being displayed upfront. I also spotted a few rare books, including an original edition of Doctor Saturday's three-volume *Traité Vaudou*, bound in human flesh. If it was signed, it was worth more than the store itself–Hell, more than the entire block.

"Who's Oya?" asked Zigor.

"It's better if you see for yourself. Besides, we don't have time for me to tell you right now. It wouldn't be polite to keep her waiting."

We walked down into a cellar cluttered with cardboard boxes. The inventory, I supposed. Gaston, with a strength one would never have expected in a centenarian, moved a few boxes out of the way, exposing a brick tunnel barely lit by a meager 60 watt bulb.

The walls were damp, reminding me of the unpleasant fact that New Orleans was, depending on the neighborhood, between ten and 100 inches below sea level.

Some claimed that Jean Lafitte had lived here in 1805; the only person who could verify that rumor was the owner herself, whom we were about to meet.

When we exited the tunnel, we walked up another flight of steps and emerged into a beautiful patio garden, which featured a profusion of sweet-smelling flowers and its own fountain where birds came to drink. It was like a beautiful oasis from out of time, one that I remembered fondly from having spent much time there as a boy.

The combination of the sights, the smells and the twittering of the birds, combined to almost overwhelm my senses. Old memories once buried, yet never forgotten, resurfaced as I tasted the air around me. The years vanished as suddenly as the birds as we crossed the patio. Suddenly, I was transported back to over 30 years earlier. Nothing had changed, except me. *She* was exactly the same.

"Hugo," she said, gratifying me with one of her enigmatic smiles. "You have become a man."

She was as beautiful, mysterious, alluring and timeless as ever. She sat in a wicker chair, sipping a mint julep from a silver goblet, leafing through the latest issue of *Vogue*.

Every time I saw her face, the thought came to me that, a long time ago, her jet-black eyes had stared into the jaws of something far worse than Death—and she hadn't blinked. Time, age and fear had no grasp on Marie Laveau. She was the mistress of all she beheld, but without pride, for pride is a stupid thing. Joy, beauty, grace and humor are what she stood for.

When she saw me, she got up and deposited two small kisses on my cheeks, like the French do. I returned the gesture. Then, I said:

"Marie, I'd like you to meet my friend Zigor Side, an attorney from the Bars of New York, Washington and California." I turned towards him and completed the introduction. "Zigor, this is Marie Laveau."

If I had said Snow-White or Princess Leia, he could not have been more surprised.

"Marie... Laveau?" he stuttered. "*The* Marie Laveau?"

It was not often that one was given an opportunity to sucker punch one of America's top lawyers. It was little joys like that that made my life worth living.

"Mr. Side," said Marie, offering her hand for a *baise-main*. The idiot took it and shook it before realizing his error.

"Gaston, bring some iced tea for Professor Van Helsing and his friend," ordered Marie.

"Marie Laveau... Wow!" whispered Zigor.

From the way he suddenly looked at me, I gathered that I had gone up, way up, in his esteem. Just as if he'd discovered that Keith Richards and I had hooked up with Patti Hansen; at the same time. Or at least, something like that.

Since he'd joined my select "Club" of Hunters, quite naturally, Zigor had improved his knowledge of the twilight world in which we moved, but he hadn't been a "virgin" when I first met him and recruited him in a Sunset Strip night club during the Second Black Dahlia case. Since then, his representation of Charlie Manson had allowed him to meet some of the a-list of the Occult, but even then, Marie Laveau, the so-called "Voodoo Queen of New Orleans," was in a class of her own.

"You've come because of Ohisver's death?" she asked.

"Yes," I replied.

"I'm sorry that your uncle and you weren't able to reconcile before..."

"So am I."

We shared a long pause during which we each evoked my uncle's memory in our own way. I remembered him as a strong, powerful man, whose face bore the traces of his many battles, and with eyes as blue as the sea on which he had spent so many years. A Burt Lancaster-type man, half-pirate, half-prophet, who was known, respected, even feared, from the jungles of Ñancahuazú in Bolivia to the *terreiros* of Bahia do Brazil. I had always thought of him as a force of nature, an unstoppable, eternal power, but when one is a child, all adults appear eternal. It is only later that we learn of the mortality and fragility of human existence.

"Have you gone to Saint-Amadou?" she finally asked.

"Not yet. Frankly, I haven't had the courage. I felt like coming here first."

She smiled discreetly, appreciating the homage I just paid her.

"So you don't know...?"

"Know what?"

"It's only gossip of course... Rumors..."

"There are no rumors in our world, Marie. As the proverb says, 'What falls inside a man's ear is heard a thousand leagues away.' What have you heard?"

"Your uncle was supposed to have taken in a partner..."

"A partner? That doesn't sound like Uncle Ohisver. He barely tolerated my father."

"A man from Haiti—who might have claims on Saint-Amadou."

"What? My uncle would never have mortgaged the House!"

"That's not what I've heard."

Suddenly, I remembered what Zigor said earlier. Could my uncle's death be suspicious after all? I decided to ask Marie for her opinion.

"Zigor wondered if the 'Massacre' might not have been the work of a rival, a jealous *houngan*, an old enemy... Uncle Ohisver made quite a few of these over the years."

"Sorry to have brought it up," added Zigor, "but in my business, every death is suspect."

Marie considered the issue while delicately taking sips of her mint julep from the silver goblet. I realized that my uncle's death did intrigue her and that she had already asked herself the very same question.

"If Ohisver's death had been caused by Voodoo," she finally said, appearing to me to be excessively cautious about her choice of words, "I would have already learned of it. Such a thing could not remain hidden from me for long." Then, after a pause, she added: "Still, I feel there is something strange in the air. *Slumbering forces have been awakened.* The *loa,* who as you know, are, terrible gossips, whisper in the wind about it. Something is definitely going on..."

"What?"

"I don't know. Not yet, anyway."

"Someone mentioned a mortgage," said Zigor, ever the practical mind. "That sort of transaction doesn't happen overnight. If it's true, we'll find legal documents at Mr. Van Helsing's house and the truth will soon be revealed."

In other words, the only way to find out what was going on was to go home to Saint-Amadou.

We got up and I said good-bye to Marie.

"We shall see each other again very soon," she whispered in my ear.

That prospect did not thrill me as I was starting to suspect that when Old Zaka had asked me to return to New Orleans at once, he wasn't just speaking of a matter of succession.

When we reentered the store, the clock tolled 5 p.m. With waiting for our luggage, the taxi ride from the airport, the nostalgic walk through the French Quarter and our chat with Marie, the afternoon had simply disappeared. One of the more wonderful characteristics of New Orleans is that, there, more than anywhere else, you don't notice the time slipping by.

Ascension turned up the volume on the radio to catch the local news.

A weather bulletin followed a dreary ad for a local mattress king. They reported that a tropical storm that had started in the Bahamas two days earlier had been officially re-classified as a hurricane. They had assigned it its name.

Katrina.

Thursday, August 25
(*Cont'd*)

THE POSSUM STEW IS READY.

Outside, it was even hotter than it had been before. It felt like a Turkish bath; the heat and humidity were suffocating. I started sweating buckets.

Zigor could no longer contain his curiosity.

"Marie Laveau... That can't be possible. It must be her great-great-granddaughter or something like that, right?"

"No," I said.

"She's *the* Marie Laveau, who was reportedly born in Haiti in 1794?"

"That's what she says, but I think she's lying..."

"I knew it!"

"...She's much older."

"What?"

"She's lived in Ancient Africa, knew the Dogon Empire, the Yoruba's secret temples in Ife, visited the lost outpost of Atlantis in the Hoggar Mountains when Antinea first moved there..."

"That can't be. Are you sure you're not mistaken?"

"Of course not; how can I be sure? But I can tell you that once, during one of our conversations, she casually mentioned that the Greek poet Krinagoras had written an epigram about her—and I found it later. It was dated from the early days of the Christian Era."

"What about the Marie Laveau who was the toast of New Orleans from 1830 to 1881, the Voodoo Queen, the great *mambo* who danced naked in the coils of Dambal-lah on the shores of Lake Pontchartrain?"

"One of her avatars, who died in 1881, to be reborn again, and again... You heard Ascension. She is Oya, the incarnation of wind, and night, and magic, the mistress of the *loa*..."

While we discussed Marie's past, we had reached Canal. From there, we caught the St. Charles streetcar and, 15 minutes later, we got off at the stop on Constantinople Street, right in the middle of the garden district.

It's the most beautiful section of New Orleans, with its old houses reeking of history, their airy verandas, fancy decorations and ornate ironwrought fences evoking the nostalgia of times long gone. Today, the tourists come to see Anne Rice's vampire Lestat's house just as they go the Château d'If to visit Edmond Dantès' cell.

A few minutes later, we turned into Jerusalem Street and finally arrived at Saint-Amadou.

The adjective that best encapsulates our family house is *old*. Saint-Amadou is not one of those houses that reeks of ancient evils and unspeakable horrors, like the House of Usher—far from it! Despite all the clinging vines and the ivy, it still looks grand. I noticed that the front garden had begun to resemble a jungle, with all the semi-tropical vegetation going wild. The weight of the passing years and the damage from tropical storms had not succeeded in completely hiding the fact that this was once a fine residence, one that could legitimately bask in its glorious past. Saint-Amadou had been beautiful 200 years ago; then, like many people, she had aged a bit, and had become a bit eccentric, maybe even a *little odd*, if one could use such terms to describe a house.

Being so old, Saint-Amadou had her share of secrets and kept visitors at bay like Gloria Swanson in *Sunset Boulevard*, seeming to say, "I'm *big*, it's the *city* that got small." But as Uncle Ohisver used to say, in our trade, success depends on word of mouth, not the shop window.

Zigor seemed impressed, and even a bit intimidated. It was the first time he'd come here. He was generally not particularly sensitive to the supernatural, yet even he could feel that this was one of those rare, special places where a normal man isn't always welcome.

"So, what do you think?" I asked with a *soupçon* of irony.

"Er, well, it's very, er, ... Yes, it sure has character, doesn't it?" he finally said.

I pushed the rusting bars of the creaking gate and we entered the property. The front garden definitely needed a squadron of gardeners to clear it. The camellias and the magnolias were involved in a no-holds-barred fight for dominance over the west side. The venerable oak that occupied the east side was in danger of being entirely swallowed up by the bane of the South, kudzu.

We climbed the three steps to the porch and arrived at the front door. On it was an ordinary brass knocker and, just above it, a small brass plate that merely said:

O. Van Helsing

I knocked twice. After a few minutes' wait, I heard the shuffling sounds of an old pair of alligator shoes that I remembered fondly, as I had bought them as a Christmas present.

The door opened and an old Haitian appeared on the doorsill. He was just as I remembered him: dressed as a Cajun farmer in *cotonade* indigo blue shirt and trousers. A profusion of religious medals hung on gold chains on his chest.

It was old Zaka, my uncle's servant and cohort on his many adventures, who used to sit me on his knees when I was a boy, and secretly bought me pralines behind my uncle's back.

"M'sieur Hugo!"

We embraced. It was the hug that I would gladly have given my uncle if fate had presented me with one last opportunity to see him again.

"M'sieur Hugo! The Saints be blessed! You're back at last! I'm so happy!"

"You know that I'd never ignore your call."

The old man was sincerely moved.

"I so wanted M'sieur Ohisver to call you, but you know how he was..."

"Stubborn as a mule. I'm afraid it's a family trait."

"Now that you're back, all that's wrong will be well again, I'm sure."

"You're going to tell me all about that, but first, let me introduce you... This is my lawyer, Zigor Side, he's come to help us... Shall we come in?"

"Yes, yes, of course. Please, come in!"

Inside, it was even hotter than outside; Hell without the air conditioning. Zaka, obviously, wasn't bothered by the suffocating heat.

We left our luggage in the hall and, purely out of habit, I walked towards the grand salon to the right.

Nothing appeared to have changed since my teens. The grand piano was still there, occupying a corner of the room. I would have bet that it still needed to be tuned. The portraits of my ancestors, who left Holland in the 17th century to seek their fortune in the New World, still hung on the walls: Kapel Van Helsing, the founding patriarch; Izak Van Helsing on Tortuga Island with Captain Blood; a century later, Yakob Van Helsing fighting alongside the *houngan* Mackandal during the revolt of the Haitian slaves of 1751; Ithamar Van Helsing and Jean Lafitte, combating shoulder to shoulder during the Battle of New Orleans in January 1815; and there was the famous duel between Rhett Butler and Aharon Van Helsing...

I made myself comfortable in a leather armchair and told Zigor to do likewise. Zaka returned with the traditional jug of ice tea. My lawyer's face grew somber. I guessed that he would have preferred something stronger.

So I got up and rummaged in the drinks cabinet. As I recalled, Uncle Ohisver liked his liquor and the current supply led me to believe that he hadn't changed in that respect. I decided to mix Zigor a Cajun Martini: three ounces of vodka, a dash of dry vermouth, ice, olives and a jalapeño pepper. With that under his belt, my lawyer would soon be the happiest attorney in the entire South.

It was now time to have a serious talk with Zaka.

"Tell me exactly what happened after Uncle Ohisver's death," I asked him. "Don't leave out any details."

The old man hesitated; words came out of his mouth painfully.

"It was a great sadness, M'sieur Hugo... I learned of M'sieur Ohisver's death when a policewoman came to tell me.... I gave her your number..."

"Yes, I know. She called me."

"They brought back all of M'sieur Ohisver's personal things. I left them in his office. Then that same night, the Haitian called..."

"What Haitian?"

"He said his name was Legendre. He saw the news on TV. It was all about the Massacre. He sounded like a lawyer. He said he had papers that made him the new owner of the House..."

"Impossible!"

Zaka shrugged, fatalistically.

"I know, M'sieur Hugo, but he seemed serious. Very polite, but serious. I told him you'd be here on Thursday. He wants to meet with you. So he said he'll be here at 7 p.m."

That left us just about an hour to get ready.

"I made dinner," Zaka added.

I was not enthused at the idea of entertaining a graverobbing shyster in my House only two days after my uncle's death, but something told me that I didn't have a choice. I had to meet the enemy, and I was better off doing it on my home turf.

"Very well. While we wait for him, we'll get settled. Is my room still vacant?"

"Of course it is, M'sieur Hugo. I've kept it just as you left it."

"Good. We'll put Zigor in Miss Patience's room then. Get some sheets and pillows while I take him up."

We grabbed our suitcases and went up the grand staircase, made of dark wood with its faded carpet smelling faintly like mildew. On the landing, there was a long corridor going to the right, one going to the left and yet another one starting behind us. Saint-Amadou always confused visitors because, as the years went by, my ancestors tinkered with the initial plan, adding a wing here, a half-floor there... It now spreads out towards the back in unexpected ways, hidden by the huge trees of our back garden. When you look at it from the front only, you don't get an accurate idea of how big it really is.

I left my suitcase in the room that used to be mine when I was a teenager. The poster for Judas Priest's *Screaming for Vengeance* was still stapled to the wall above the bed. I took Zigor to his room, at the end of the corridor, before returning to my room.

I'm ridin', ridin' on the wind... I had fallen asleep. I had dreamed of Judas Priest's metal bird screaming vengeance like a demon in the sky. Something big, something powerful was coming... Something that was going to burst upon us like a thunderclap, heralding death and fates worse than death...

I felt in a particularly black mood. I used the adjacent bathroom to freshen up and splash some water on my face. I looked tired. My travel clock told me it was almost 7 p.m. so it was time to go down for dinner.

Zaka had laid a table for three in the formal dining room. It wasn't the most friendly room in the House since Uncle Ohisver had redecorated it with all kinds of Santeria junk he had brought back from Cuba before Castro... But that is a story for another time...

I have seen people with very solid stomachs refuse to eat Zaka's Cajun-style possum stew while looking at a portrait of Babaly Ayé, the *orisha* of filth and disease. Perhaps it was my uncle's way of discouraging too much entertaining at home?

Zaka was still busy in the kitchen when the doorbell rang. He wiped his hands and prepared to go and let our guest in when I gestured to him to stay and finish his preparations.

I opened the door myself and discovered a tall mulatto on the other side, dressed in a classy *sur mesure* three-piece suit that would not have looked out of place on Wall Street. He held a black leather briefcase and wore designer sunglasses—it was still rather bright outside. I couldn't tell his reaction at seeing me.

"Professor Van Helsing?" he inquired with a bright Colgate smile, holding his hand.

I shook it. It was a firm handshake, with no quarter given on either side.

"I'm Hugo Van Helsing. You must be Monsieur Legendre?"

"I am indeed. I am sorry that we have to meet under such tragic circumstances..."

I nodded and invited him in.

"Your uncle was more than a business associate..." he continued.

At that moment, I heard Zigor rushing down the stairs. He, too, had fallen asleep, and he looked even more disheveled than usual. I bet he'd had a few nightmares.

"Ah," I said, "this is my attorney, Mr. Zigor Side of the New York Bar, whom I asked to come with me to help me untangle my uncle's succession."

Legendre and Zigor looked at each other like two boxing champs, each trying to measure the other's strength. There would be no love lost between the two. Zigor couldn't stand prim and proper businessmen, all conceit and righteousness, and to the Haitian, I thought he must have looked like one of those *dirty f*** hippies* who still polluted America's precious bodily fluids.

"I should say that, until today, I was completely in the dark about you, Monsieur Legendre," I said, hoping to score a point.

He smiled enigmatically. I found it irritating.

"I brought with me (he shook his briefcase) all the necessary documents to bring you up to date, Professor."

"We'll have plenty of time to discuss this after dinner," I said, leading him towards the dining room. "I believe Zaka has prepared us one of his Cajun specialties..."

Inside, I prayed that he hadn't made his utterly revolting possum stew.

"The possum stew is ready," said Zaka, coming out of the kitchen with a big smile. "You may sit down."

I had attended many more convivial dinner parties in my time. I remembered, for instance, dining with Fen-Chu the night before his execution by the Chinese after they took over Macao in 1999, and the ambiance was significantly more cheerful.

Our guest's conversation was anything but inspiring. Apparently, Legendre had somehow been involved with Baby Doc Duvalier's government and had managed to land back on his feet with Jean-Bertrand Aristide when, in 1994, the Americans intervened to throw out the junta of General Cédras, who had overthrown him three years earlier.

Legendre's stories were an odd mix of old war buddies' stories and *Tales from the Crypt*. They wouldn't have been to everyone's taste, but they went well with the frightful decor—and Zaka's appalling possum stew.

Zigor, ever the pragmatic attorney, seized the first opportunity that presented itself to start the interrogation. I can't say that I minded. Haiti's recent history was more like a bloody kaleidoscope of horrors than a diorama for school children. I felt that he had been waiting impatiently for that opportunity for a while.

"Mr. Legendre," he started, "am I guessing correctly that the goal of all your very entertaining stories is to prepare us for the reasons for your association with the late Ohisver van Helsing?"

Legendre smiled, or tried to. His smile reminded me of that of the Joker in the *Batman* comics I used to read.

"Guilty as charged, Mr. Side! Despite this excellent dinner..." (I couldn't stand the sarcasm) "...I guess that your client is understandably impatient to find out what brought me here. Well, I'm only too happy to enlighten you both... As soon as your servant clears the table," he finished with a somewhat contemptuous look, throwing his rumpled napkin to the floor. Zaka's pained expression made me hate Legendre even more. But I needed to control myself and appear calm.

"You wish to know the nature of my business relationship with your late uncle?" he continued, turning towards me. "It's quite normal—and very simple. In 1994, after the US intervention we were just talking about, the Aristide government decided to relaunch the exploitation of some long-abandoned gold mines that exist in our northern peninsula, and to finance that business by calling on American gold traders—gold bugs, as they're called. However, as is often the case in the Caribbean, they made it a condition that these speculators should be partnered with local interests. An *ad hoc* company was set up for that purpose: the Haitian-American Development Corporation. Thanks to my good relations with the Aristide Government, I became one of the bankers admitted into the pool set up to finance the venture. That's how I became partner with about a dozen American investors, including your uncle, who had invested a sizeable sum, financed by my bank, and put up this house as collateral..."

"I didn't know anything about this."

"I understand that you and your uncle had been estranged for some time. It is not unusual that, under such circumstances..."

"We will want to see a copy of the mortgage note and any documents pertaining to the loan made to Mr. Van Helsing," said Zigor.

"Of course. As I said, I've brought everything with me. I'll leave you with a copy of the file."

He didn't take offense at Zigor's request, but then being a banker; he must have been used to his clients suspecting him of the worst.

"And whatever happened to this wonderful investment opportunity?" I asked. "I don't recall reading anything in the papers about new gold mines in Haiti."

"You are correct, Professor. In 2005, when the Aristide government was in turn overthrown, the mechanics of what was revealed to be a confidence trick, as old as the world, were exposed. I hurry to add, because I can guess what you're thinking—please, don't deny it, it's perfectly understandable!—that I, myself, lost a not inconsiderable amount of money in the affair. In fact, I had to close my bank. But I inherited your uncle's note. Since Mr. Van Helsing had always been completely trustworthy with me in the past, I didn't feel any pressure as I knew that he would eventually repay me, as in fact he had been doing these last few years. Then, a few days ago, I saw on CNN that he had been one of the unfortunate victims of that abominable massacre... You understand now why I felt it was important that I come here in person, first and foremost to offer you my sincerest condolences, but also—and please excuse my frankness—to make my claim known."

"I see."

Legendre pulled out a thick file from his briefcase and put it delicately down in the table.

"I do not think you will find anything out of order, Mr. Side," he said, addressing himself to Zigor. "Most of the legal work was done by a local firm, at your uncle's request. They're located not too far from here, I believe. Hamilton & Hamilton, on St. Charles."

Zigor grabbed the file and started looking through it. His occasional *tsk tsk* led me to believe that Legendre must have been telling the truth and that our position was not very good.

"I understand that you would want to retain ownership of this wonderful old house which has been in your family for generations, Professor," said Legendre. "We Haitians are very respectful of traditions. I would not want to force you to sell. You uncle had collected a certain number of religious artifacts over the years. That is, in fact, how we met, for I share the same passion. I might be interested in doing a trade... We might be able to arrive at a mutually satisfactory compromise without any lawyers or messy legal procedures..."

I smelled a trap somewhere, but I had no idea where.

"I'll think about it," I replied.

"I understand, but if I might be allowed to give you a piece of advice, dictated purely by the friendship that I had with your uncle, do not take too much time. *Slumbering forces have been awakened.*"

I winced. This was exactly what Marie Laveau had said earlier.

"I will not impose upon your hospitality any longer in what must be, I'm sure, a very painful time for you. Could I ask you to call me a taxi? I'm staying at the Fairmont. I'll call you again on Saturday morning after

you have had time to review the matter more compre-
hensively..."

He got up and walked towards the front door while
Zaka was calling for a cab. Less than a minute later, a
Crescent City car pulled up by the curb.

"Professor Van Helsing, Mr. Side, it was pleasure."

Legendre shook our hands one last time before
walking away into the night.

I closed the door softly behind the Haitian.

"What do you make of it?" I asked Zigor.

"I've got to study the file, but on the surface of it, I
think it looks legit. I don't think you've got a leg to
stand on. If you want to keep this house, you might be
better off negotiating a side deal."

"I see that, but what if it's not the House that he's
after? What does he *really* want then?"

Zigor shook his head. He had no more clue than I
did.

It was about 2 a.m. when I suddenly woke up with a
start, my mind perfectly clear. It was as if a bell had
tolled inside my head.

It happened to me once in a while, and it was never
a good sign.

I knew that I hadn't been awakened by a normal
noise, because the House was totally silent. As the saying goes, not a creature was stirring.

The air was heavy, muggy; through the open windows, the night carried with it the smells of the incoming
storm and the sweet scent of the eucalyptus.

I opened the door and stepped into the corridor.

Nothing.

I softly walked down the stairs. Zaka's room was near the garden; to leave, Zigor would have had to walk past my door, so I couldn't have heard either of them.

If I actually had heard something.

What I perceived was not an outside entity, whose presence might have been unconsciously detected by one of my five senses, but something that I felt came from inside me.

Once on the ground floor, I turned right to go into Uncle Ohisver's office-cum-library. The moonlight coming through the bay windows cast a ghostly pall upon the room. Still guided by my inner voice, I pressed on a hidden stud between two bookshelves, causing one to swing open, revealing a narrow stone staircase descending into the cellars of Saint-Amadou.

Since my uncle's death, only Zaka and I knew the secret of this hidden passage designed by my ancestor, Ithamar Van Helsing who built Saint-Amadou. He was a man whose business could have had him swinging at the nasty end of a rope several times in his life, and undoubtedly, he had thought it wise to leave himself an escape route.

I walked down the stairs, following a music that I was the only one to hear.

Here and there, small slits were pierced into the walls, enabling one to spy on the cellars themselves.

They looked like the stock room of a mad antique collector—or, less kindly, a junkyard in an advanced stage of decay. There was a hodgepodge collection of furniture and objects accumulated by Uncle Ohisver during a life of travels. Here was a suit of medieval Japanese armor. Next to it were two crates labeled *Nicaragua*. Everywhere were piles of religious artifacts, from Alaska to Tierra Del Fuego. I saw boxes and boxes of books stashed in rows against the walls. In a corner, there were three pirate chests that looked like they ought to be full of gold doubloons and precious stones—maybe they were.

Suddenly, I noticed the roving light of a lamptorch flickering between the boxes. It was getting closer. In a few seconds, I would discover the identity of our mysterious nocturnal visitor.

It was Legendre!

So he had returned and surreptitiously found his way into our cellars. It couldn't have been very hard to break the lock on our back gate, or maybe he had used the underground tunnel that connects the cellars to the Lafayette Cemetery, not far from here. He could have learned its existence from my uncle; God knows what other secrets of ours he might have ferreted out...

The Haitian was searching the cellars methodically, obviously looking for something special. Perhaps I was finally going to learn what he was really after.

Suddenly, my attention was caught not by the torchlight he held in his right hand, but by what he had in the other. Something that shone with a supernatural radiance and whose ethereal vibrations pounded my brain with rhythmic, increasing pain.

I squinted my eyes to better see what it was, as if I was trying to read the small print on the back of an insurance contract.

It turned out to be an African-style dagger with an ebony handle and an ivory blade with strange carvings. Its pommel ended with a double-axe decorated with silver inlays.

As I focused on the object, Legendre stopped and unexpectedly turned towards the wall behind which I was hiding, as if he had guessed my presence there—but how could he have done so, since we were separated by a thick stone wall?

He stepped forward, holding the dagger high in the air, as if it were a standard.

Behind him, above him, through him—I don't know how I can describe this sensation any more accurately—I perceived the presence of something terrifying, an awesome entity that emanated directly from the dagger. Someone, something compared to which I was nothing and less than nothing.

I knew then that I stood in the presence of a God.

The pounding in my head kept growing stronger. I barely had time to whisper the Raaaee Incantation that protects the mind—and the soul!—of mortals from harmful contacts with the Unspeakable Ones, before I found solace in what H. P. Lovecraft called the *irradiate refuge of sleep.*[3]

---

[3] When the last days were upon me, and the ugly trifles of existence began to drive me to madness like the small drops of water that torturers let fall ceaselessly upon one spot of their victim's body, I loved the irradiate refuge of sleep. *Ex Oblivione.*

Friday, August 26

EVERY BANKER IS SOMETHING OF A SORCERER.

I woke up in my bed.

I decided to postpone seeking answers to the questions that sprang to mind until later. After taking a shower and putting on a lighter set of clothes—it was already uncomfortably hot—I went downstairs. Nine o'clock had just rung on the grandfather clock in the vestibule.

In the dining room, I found Zaka serving Zigor his morning cup of coffee. My attorney seemed well-rested. I bet he had slept like a dormouse. He was reading Robert Sheckley's *Dimension of Miracles Revisited* when he saw me enter. He noticed the expression on my face and put down his book.

"What's wrong?" he asked.

Perceptive as ever.

I started telling him the story of my nocturnal meanderings. As I reached the end, Zaka butted in:

"I'm the one who put you back to bed, M'sieur Hugo."

To say I was surprised would be an understatement.

"Where was I? What happened?"

"There was a ring at the door..."

"I can verify that," said Zigor. "I heard it. It must have been around 6 a.m."

"...I'd just begun to make the preparations for breakfast. I went to open it and it was the Haitian..."

"Legendre?"

"Yes. He was holding you up as if you were drunk or passed out."

"What did he say?"

"He said that he'd found you like that outside. He didn't say where exactly, but he asked me to tell you to avoid underground tunnels in the future. The damp is bad for your health. Ah! And he also wanted me to tell you that he's ready to *exchange the keys* whenever you are."

"*Exchange the keys*? What did he mean by that?"

"I don't know anything more, M'sieur Hugo. He dropped you into my arms and he left."

"Perhaps he does want Saint-Amadou after all?" said Zigor.

"But why go through such a charade if that's the case?"

"No idea, but at least we know where to start..."

Zigor grabbed the thick folder of documents left behind by Legendre the night before.

"I've gone through the file, but there are still a few obscure points that I'd like to clarify. Since Hamilton & Hamilton is nearby, I suggest we go and pay them a little visit."

Half-an-hour later, after having walked up to St. Charles and down the avenue towards Canal, we arrived at a small storefront law office located just near the Lafayette Hotel. It looked like a neighborhood family practice, with the name painted in green letters on the storefront.

We went in; there was no receptionist to greet us. We found ourselves in a rather sad little office, filled with archive boxes and decorated with a single, anemic-looking potted plant.

Zigor and I looked at each other, underwhelmed by the décor.

"Anyone home?" I said loudly.

A young, blond, athletic-looking man, with an open face, came out of the back. He was dressed in a polo shirt and slacks and carried a file box.

"Sorry, but I'm all alone today, and a bit over-whelmed," he said. "Can I help you?"

"We'd like to see Mr. Hamilton," I said.

"I'm Jonathan Hamilton. And you are...?"

"Professor Hugo Van Helsing. I've come to inquire about the estate of my uncle, Ohisver Van Helsing. This is my attorney, Mr. Zigor Side of New York."

"Ah, yes, I knew your uncle, of course. What a tragedy! Please come into my office."

Jonathan invited us to follow him. We walked down a corridor leading to two offices, a kitchenette and a supply room. File boxes were stashed against the walls, all the way up to the ceiling.

"I apologize for the mess. We're, er, moving."

We went into the smaller of the two offices. It was cluttered with paperwork. Jonathan cleared two chairs and invited us to sit down.

Zigor started right off the bat.

"My client was informed yesterday by a Haitian banker named Legendre that he held a promissory note collateralized by a mortgage on Saint-Amadou, his late uncle's house. Here is a copy of the note and the mort-gage documents. It was prepared by your firm as part of an investment package purporting to exploit some gold mines in Northern Haiti. Are you familiar with this mat-ter?"

Jonathan took the documents and quickly leafed through them.

"I see... Naturally, the market value of your house today is vastly greater than that of the original loan, which I see here was made in 1994—possibly twice as much. If you sold the house, it would be easy to repay Mr. Legendre. Or alternatively, I'm sure you could easily find another bank willing to refinance the original mortgage..."

"I wish neither to sell nor remortgage Saint-Amadou," I said as categorically as possible.

"And, er, excuse me for asking, but your own personal finances are not sufficient to...?"

"Not at the present, I'm afraid."

"My client isn't seeking to avoid his responsibilities," said Zigor. "But you will understand that this transaction, of which he was entirely unaware, came rather as a shock. To speak frankly, we wish to make sure that we're not the victims of some kind of scam."

"I understand," said Jonathan, before pausing for a second. "I must tell you that it was my father, Richard Hamilton, who took care of Mr. Van Helsing's business, and therefore, I'm not nearly as familiar with the details of his file..."

"You said, 'who took care?' "

"My father is dead. I wasn't entirely honest with you before. We're not moving, I've decided to close the practice. My father's ambition was for me to take over someday, but we didn't share the same goals. Family law, divorces, small-time bankruptcies... I don't feel that that's why I went to Law School. I'd rather work for a big firm. In fact, I've already had several attractive offers..."

The remorse I read on his face at the notion of disappointing a dead parent suddenly made this young attorney seem much more sympathetic. We were both confronted with the same impossible, parental demands, and now faced the same unenviable regrets.

"Is there anything you can remember that might enable us to challenge this note?" asked Zigor.

"I haven't finished packing all of my father's files. I'll have another look, of course, but off hand, I can't think of anything... Unless... I remember one meeting that took place here between Mr. Van Helsing and Mr. Legendre. I sat through it to take notes because my father's secretary was out sick that day..."

"And...?"

"I recall that during that meeting, Mr. Legendre had been insistent on acquiring some kind of antiquity that your uncle had in his possession... Something of great value which, now that I think of it, might offer you a bargaining chip..."

"Do you remember what it was?"

"Hmmm... A *key*, I think. Does that ring a bell?"

Zigor and I exchanged a look. Legendre had told Zaka that he was *ready to exchange the keys...* Were we on the right trail at last?

"No, I can't say that it does," I replied.

"Too bad. Listen, come back tomorrow at the same time. Between now and then, I'll have had time to search through my father's records and if I find something, anything at all, I'll be only too happy to assist you."

Once again, we found ourselves outside, walking down St. Charles towards Canal.

"I think that last night, Legendre was looking for that 'key,' whatever it is, in the cellars," I said.

"So I was right after all. Something's rotten in the Kingdom of Denmark," said Zigor.

51

"I concede the point. We need to start right back at the beginning. I'm going to try to find out what my uncle's 'key' might be, and why it's at the center of this whole mess. Why don't you call Citrin and ask him to..."

"Do I have to?" whined Zigor. "I hate dealing with that guy. He's a merc and he stinks. I mean that literally. Have you gotten a whiff of him lately?"

"It's not his fault. He developed some kind of glandular condition after 9/11. But if I were you, I'd keep my opinions to myself. You know how sensitive he is..."

I didn't need to say anymore. No man with a sane mind would want to purposefully incur the wrath of James Citrin. I continued:

"Citrin has some high-ranking contacts at the NSA. We need someone like him to run a thorough search on Legendre and turn up everything there is to know about him."

"Humph," said Zigor; it was a grumbling noise that I chose to interpret as a sign of consent. "My firm has a correspondent in New Orleans. Mike something or other. I've met him once; he's a swell guy and very helpful. They've got Lexis and all the bells and whistles there. I'll squat in his conference room and start doing some research."

"OK, and I'll go back and see Marie. I have the definite feeling that she knows what this 'key' business is all about."

"Cool. So we'll meet back at Saint-Amadou?"

"Yes. Let's say around 5 p.m."

"See you later, alligator."

Zigor grabbed a passing streetcar and I was simply left alone on the sidewalk.

It was about time for lunch and I decided to treat myself at Brennan's on Royal in the French Quarter.

There, I found out from a waitress that the chef, Michael Roussel, an old friend of mine, was long retired and, in fact, had recently passed away. Michael had taken over the restaurant from Paul Blange in 1977. This was yet another fragment of my youth that, like an iceberg, was detaching itself from the present to float away and vanish into the dark waters of the past. I ordered the traditional Eggs Hussarde with a Creole Bloody Mary, but despite the sunny atmosphere of the patio, the joy of the moment had gone.

I ended my meal with Bananas Foster; Brennan's still serves the best Bananas Foster in New Orleans. Then, after I had finished my meal, I walked to Marie Laveau's occult shop.

Ascension stood behind the counter just as she had the day before.

"Professor Van Helsing!" She greeted me with her wonderful smile. "I didn't think I'd have the pleasure of seeing you back so soon."

"The pleasure is all mine, Miss Proudfoot."

"Please, call me Ascension."

"Ascension, I need to speak with Marie. Is she here?"

The young woman looked at the clock.

"Right now, she's in consultation with Mrs. Garth, but she should be done soon."

"I'll wait then. Tell her it's urgent. I have to see her as soon as she's free."

To while away the time, I began looking at the collection of items that had been gathered on the shelves in the backroom. The real stuff, as I said. In addition to Dr. Saturday's Treatise, which I'd noticed before, I saw two amazing paintings by Rowley Thorne, a copy of Etienne-Laurent de Marigny's notebooks describing his travels on the island of Saint-Sebastian, and an old four-track Nagra tape which was a recording of Jimi Hendrix's original version of *Voodoo Chile*, made at the Scene in New York during his famous jam session with Steve Winwood and Jack Casaday.

There was no price sticker on it. I wondered how much Marie wanted for it. More than my soul was worth, very likely.

"Oya will see you now, Professor," said Ascension.

"Call me Hugo. After all, we're, er, cousins."

She blushed.

I followed Gaston who quickly led me to the Voodoo Queen of New Orleans.

"Hugo. Back so soon. Did you find out some new information about your uncle's death?" she asked, not seeming too surprised.

"Yes."

I gave her a fairly detailed report of what Zigor and I had learned to date.

"Legendre," she cut in at one point. "I've heard of him. His grandfather was 'Murder' Legendre, an evil *houngan* who terrorized Haiti in the 1930s. If the rumors are true, his grandson is even worse."

"He claims to be a banker."

"Every banker is something of a sorcerer," she said, smiling. "But do go on. What does he want?"

I told her about my nocturnal encounter in the cellars of Saint-Amadou. When I mentioned the strange, shining knife that Legendre held, she reacted with horror and put down her silver goblet.

"Describe that knife, describe it precisely," she said, alarmed.

I did so, focusing on the strange pommel with its twin axe.

"The Dagger of Hevioso!" she blurted out.

"What?"

Her eyes suddenly grew distant, gazing back into the mists of a past that was unremembered by any other man or woman living on Earth today.

"Oya was born in Ancient Africa, the ancestral birthplace of humanity, amongst the tribes of what is today called Dahomey, whose children's children were later taken by slavers to the far lands of Haiti and the New World..."

I couldn't tell if she was talking about herself in the third person or someone else; I wondered if she even knew herself.

"Oya was the high priestess of the *Vodun* Gods, for in those ancient times, the Gods walked amongst the children of men, sharing their passions and shaping their legends. Four of the Gods created four powerful, magical talismans, which they each gave to their own priest or priestess, conferring upon these a fraction of their great powers, making them not unlike an earthly incarnation of the Gods... Thus did Oya receive as gift the Cup of Erzulie, the Goddess of Love and Vengeance, which can transform any liquid poured into it into the most powerful of love potions... Shango received the Dagger of Hevioso, the God of Thunder and Lightning, which has the power to control the sky and the elements... Wedo was offered the Medallion of Damballah, the Lord of Serpents and the Master of the Loa... And last, Sogbo was given the greatest and deadliest gift of all, the Key of Sakbata, from he whom is called 'Baron Samedi,' the God of Death and Decay, whose talisman can pry open the gates between Life and Death... As the sands of time flowed, the Gods grew tired of this mortal sphere and retired to the Undying Lands to live with

Mawu-Lisa, the Mother and Father of All, but they left their four talismans behind, which still conferred upon their owners the powers of the Gods who had created them."

"Legendre is an evil *houngan* who has managed to get his hands on the Dagger of Hevioso?"

"It seems so. It is said that it was the power of that talisman which buttressed the regime of Papa Doc Duvalier for so long, and that his son, Baby Doc, inherited it, then sold it to a wealthy Swiss collector during his exile in Europe, but they say so many things..."

"Don't tell me that you haven't kept track of the talismans. You are not called the Voodoo Queen for nothing."

"Age has made you smarter, Hugo," she replied with a wicked smile. "But you have an exaggerated opinion of my powers."

"Legendre obviously seeks the other three talismans. What do you know about them?"

"The Medallion is gone, no one knows where. There are many stories about it. Some claim that it was once in the possession of the serial killer Charles Lee Ray, others swear they saw it hanging around the neck of the *houngan* Papa Shorty... The Cup is reputed to have been melted down by the sinister Armand Loucque, but I don't believe that, because I don't think any mortal could destroy something created by a God... As for the Key of Baron Samedi, it belonged to the notorious Buonaparte Ignace Gallia, before falling into the hands of your uncle..."

"Uncle Ohisver?" I was stunned to learn of this. I knew that my uncle had collected some odd and powerful artifacts during his adventure-filled life, but it had never occurred to me that he might have gotten his hands on something that held the power of life and death.

"Don't look at me like that, Hugo," said Marie. "You're the one who first brought up what Legendre said about *exchanging the keys*. It's obvious that he wants to trade you Saint-Amadou for the Key of Sakbata."

"But I don't know where it is. Uncle Ohisver never even told me he had it."

"You weren't talking to each other. He probably believed that if you didn't want to walk the path of your ancestors, then you shouldn't be burdened with such a secret."

I felt a very deep and painful regret that my uncle had died without learning that I had become a worthy successor. By hiding the secret of the Key from me, he had taken on a burden which, in all likelihood, had caused his death. I was now convinced that Zigor had been right in thinking that Ohisver's death had been the result of foul play.

"If the Key had been in Saint-Amadou's cellars, Legendre would have found it," I said, now approaching the problem with a more analytical angle. "Uncle Ohisver must have hidden it somewhere else. But where?"

"I don't know," said Marie. "Had he insisted on telling me, I would have refused to listen. If anyone believed that Marie Laveau controlled the power of the Key of Sakbata, it would quickly start a war amongst the practitioners of Voodoo. No, I'm afraid this secret is yours and yours alone, Hugo. It is your duty to find the Key and, whatever else happens, to make sure that it does not fall into the hands of someone like Legendre. The fate of the world may well rest upon it."

At 3:50 p.m., I was back at Saint-Amadou. Zaka was already busy in the kitchen preparing the evening's meal. From the smells, I guessed that he was cooking his own version of the *gumbo saya* soup, into which everything that runs, crawls or jumps in a Cajun barnyard finds its final destination.

"Zaka, I have a question for you," I asked.

"Yes, M'sieur Hugo?" he said, wiping his hand rather pointlessly on a dirty rag.

"I found out what Legendre was looking for last night in the cellars: the Key of Sakbata...."

Upon hearing the name of the dreaded Baron Samedi, the old man crossed himself several times and plunged his hand deep inside the collection of religious medals hanging on his chest.

"...Which apparently my uncle had in his possession. Do you know anything about it?"

"No, M'sieur Hugo."

"Come on, my uncle had no secrets from you... Do you remember Patience Latrelle who stayed with us for a while?"

"Yes, she's in Shanghai now. She sent me a card for Christmas."

"Then you probably also remember her 'protector,' Buonaparte Ignace Gallia, who sometimes claimed he was the incarnation of Baron Samedi (Zaka crossed himself again) and who killed Ruven Van Helsing, my uncle's father. Did he have the key? Is that how my uncle got it?"

"I don't know, M'sieur Hugo."

He genuinely seemed not to know anything about it. The solution to the mystery, I was certain, lay in the past; a past that included me, but only as an indifferent witness to what was happening around me at the time.

Not only was I indifferent, but was perhaps even a bit hostile. I understood better why Uncle Ohisver hadn't felt it wise to share his secrets with an adolescent who had only a very limited interest in matters pertaining to the Occult.

In the same way, I couldn't help feeling that, for Zaka, I was still the young "M'sieur Hugo" who he had known 20 years ago. I had to make a conscious effort to shake off the tendrils of that past, which seemed to constantly try to pull me back. They permeated every inch of Saint-Amadou, from the smells of the kitchen to the metallic sounds of Judas Priest, which still played inside my head.

I had to get a grip. If I lost my edge, the consequences might be grim, as Marie had hinted at earlier. Suddenly, I remembered something else Zaka had said the previous night, that the police had returned my uncle's personal effects, and which were still in the library.

I decided to search them. Perhaps they held the clue that would lead me to the key.

I had spread everything out on top of the ancient oak desk that had once belonged to the Mayfair witches. But there appeared to be nothing that was out of the ordinary there. I looked at my uncle's wallet with his driver's license, his medical insurance card, a few credit card receipts, a hotel bill folded around a magnetic card, three business cards (his doctor, optometrist and dentist), a lotto ticket, his lucky charm that had been a present from Mamaloa Edmonds (and which nevertheless failed to save his life) and 22 dollars and 18 cents in cash. Plus a macabre spot of dried blood that reminded me of his grisly end.

I decided to search the desk drawers. There, too, I didn't find anything relevant, even in the one drawer locked with a key, hidden under an ashtray. There were three checkbooks, a savings passbook, a stash of monthly statements from his broker and a personal invitation to a conference by Dr. Jericho Drumm.

I started going through the pentaflex files that Uncle Ohisver had accumulated over the years with the intention of someday writing a book about New Orleans' occult history. *Sic transit gloria mundi!*

After a good hour of unquestionably fascinating reading, I was still no closer to finding anything useful about the possible location of the Key of Sakbata.

It was by then almost 5 p.m., so I decided to take a break and put on the local news. I grabbed the remote and turned on the TV. The news was all about Hurricane Katrina.

It seemed that things had gotten worse, much worse, during the last 24 hours. The eye of the hurricane had mysteriously moved west. The computer models had now shifted the potential path of Katrina 150 miles westward from the Florida Panhandle, putting New Orleans right in the center of their track probabilities. This scenario was a potential catastrophe, because 80% of the city was below sea level. We were told that Governor Kathleen Blanco had just proclaimed a State of Emergency and had asked the Pentagon for troop assistance.

It looked incredibly serious.

But then, I thought that Saint-Amadou and New Orleans were used to hurricanes. Some of the bars in the French Quarter even remained open all night during them to give those who dared defy the elements yet another opportunity to celebrate their zest for life.

So I chose to remain cautiously optimistic. I couldn't have been more wrong.

Zigor returned at around 6 p.m. and I immediately recognized the expression on his face: it was that of the kid who had found a stash of rare comics in his neighbor's dustbin. Obviously, his afternoon had been as productive as mine.

I decided to let him enjoy his moment of glory.

"So?" I asked.

"I didn't waste my time," he said, sounding pleased.

"Neither did I, but you go first."

He pulled out a well-worn spiral notebook from his pocket and began reading from his scribbled notes.

"I started right at the beginning," he said, "i.e.: the so-called *Massacre of Napoleon Avenue*, as the papers called it, where your uncle was shot. The local press, unlike our national media, was less preoccupied with the sensationalism of its coverage so they managed to dig up some interesting bits of news. For instance, the shooter..."

"Frank Clayton?"

"Yeah... Frank was obsessed by a new video game called *Armageddon IV*..."

"I think I heard that on CNN. Video games have replaced comic books and rock 'n roll as the perfect scapegoat for our times. It's just as stupid now as it was then."

"I agree, but in this case, two of Frank's nerdy friends, who may have been trying to somehow find an excuse for his behavior, or maybe were trying to ease their own consciences, wrote on a blog that Frank had been given a beta version of the game by the manufacturer. Apparently, he was a well-known figure in the gaming community and that kind of thing is pretty common. The player tests the game at no cost to the manufacturer, and if he likes it, the word-of-mouth alone can generate sizeable pre-sales. Anyway, two friends of Frank's swore that it was that beta version, that no one else ever saw, that had driven Frank over the edge..."

"That seems pretty unbelievable."

Meanwhile, Zaka had begun to serve his *gumbo* in large soup plates decorated with fleur-de-lis. We began eating and worshipped in mutual and respectful silence at the altar of Cajun cuisine, of which Zaka was a high priest.

After finishing the generous helping that the old man had served him, Zigor pulled his notebook back out and continued:

"I thought the notion that Frank Clayton had been somehow driven to commit mass murder by a video game was preposterous too, but you know me, I don't like to leave any stones unturned, so I decided to check out the manufacturer, just to put the whole thing to rest. It turns out that it's a small software company located in Montreal, nothing out of the ordinary, except that its name is SIMBI—it stands for SIMulations Binaires Limitée..."

"*Simbi*... The cosmic serpent of the Voodoo pantheon... OK, I agree that's odd, but a lot of game manufacturers like to use names drawn from various mythologies. It's a coincidence."

"Is it also a coincidence that SIMBI belongs to the Haitian-American Development Corporation?"

"But isn't that the name of...?"

"Yep. The company whose banker was, or maybe still is, Legendre, and which is the reason for the promissory note that your uncle signed—something I expect to be confirmed if young Mr. Hamilton finds copies of the supporting documents that were given to your uncle to persuade him to invest in said company."

"So you're saying that Uncle Ohisver was shot by a young man whose mind was manipulated..."

"Allegedly manipulated."

"...Was allegedly manipulated by a company which, in fact, has business ties to Legendre..."

"Yep, that about sums it up all right."

"...Who is an evil *houngan* who seeks the Key of Sakbata, which my uncle had in his possession."

"Ah-ha! I see that you haven't been wasting your day either! Go on, tell me more!"

I knew that nothing excited Zigor more than the thrill of the hunt; the search for clues to solve a mystery. So I quickly gave him a summary of Marie's more pertinent revelations.

"So Legendre may have used this rather convoluted but untraceable method to get rid of your uncle and gain leverage against you, his heir, to force you to surrender that Key-thing."

"That's what it looks like, but there's a glitch. I have no idea where Uncle Ohisver hid the Key."

"Which in any event, you wouldn't want Legendre to have."

"That goes without saying. He already is in possession of the Dagger of Hevioso..."

"Remind me, what is he's the God of, your José?"

"Hevioso..."

Suddenly, it was as if a blinding sun had pierced through the clouds of my mind.

In unison, we turned round to look at the TV which continued to bombard us with news about the hurricane which now threatened Louisiana.

"The God of Thunder and Lightning, which has the power to control the sky and the elements," I said, feeling a yawning pit in the bottom of my stomach.

"Well, it looks to me like that mortgage may not be his sole leverage after all," concluded Zigor in a weak voice.

Saturday, August 27

THE GODS DO EXIST. AND THEY ARE EVIL.

It was about 5 a.m. when I woke up bathed in sweat. The bedsheets were soaked. The weather was so hot and the humidity so high that I couldn't sleep any longer. The fans only served to churn out more warm air in a monsoon-like atmosphere that reminded me of my trips to Thailand.

I turned on the small TV set in my bedroom, which, surprisingly, still worked after all these years. I had watched many a late night movie on it.

According to the weathermen on CNN, Katrina had just been upgraded to a Category 3 Hurricane—meaning winds of up to 130 mph. The experts seemed rather non-plussed by the rapid progression of the storm, but they didn't know what I knew.

I drank a glass of cool water while listening distractedly to the catastrophic scenarios that were being almost gleefully laid out by the commentators. Not all ghouls slept in crypts, I thought.

The authorities were talking about evacuating the city.

I decided to take a Xanax before going back to bed, while reciting William Morris' *The Haystack in the Floods*. One or the other was usually enough to guarantee a decent night's sleep, but the two together were an invincible combination.

When I opened my eyes again, it was 8:30 a.m. and, notwithstanding the facile effects of horror novelists, I hadn't had any nightmares; in fact, I felt remarkably refreshed. Modern medicine had worked its miracle again, unless it was good ol' William Morris.

An hour or so later, after a rushed breakfast, Zigor and I arrived at Jonathan Hamilton's office. He greeted us as warmly as he had the day before.

"I've got some good news for you," he said, after we'd settled in. "I found a copy of the original investment prospectus, as well as the various releases and other notarized documents signed by your uncle."

He spread a dozen pieces of paper on the desk and Zigor descended upon them like a vulture looking for fresh meat.

Yes, the company that had been in charge of the exploitation of the alleged gold mines in Northern Haiti was indeed the Haitian-American Development Corporation!

I swore between my teeth and Zigor whistled softly, almost unconsciously, as he always did when he found the legal equivalent of a smoking gun. Of course, Jonathan noticed our reactions at once.

"Anything wrong?" he inquired.

Zigor and I looked briefly at each other, then I nodded, and we began telling the young lawyer the nature and extent of our suspicions.

"...So," I finished, "it looks increasingly possible that Legendre was behind the massacre that took my uncle's life."

Jonathan suddenly became very pale.

"I need to tell you something that I hadn't thought I should mention to you before," he said. "I told you that my father, Richard, had just died, but I didn't tell you when and how. Like your uncle, he was one of Frank Clayton's victims that day."

I was a little surprised that he hadn't mentioned that fact the day before when I had described the particulars of my uncle's death. It seemed to me that, if you lose a parent in such tragic circumstances, you would naturally want to talk about it... But I was a total stranger, after all, a foreigner even, so why should he have?

"If your Legendre is responsible for my father's death," he added, "I want to do anything in my power to help you bring him to justice."

"You're not serious," I said.

"Yes, I am."

"With all due respect, Mr. Hamilton, you're not, er, shall we say, equipped to help us effectively in our task."

"Yesterday, I've made some inquiries about you, Professor Van Helsing, and you too, Mr. Side. While I admit that I don't have any experience in your particular field, nevertheless, I believe I can be of help. I'm a member of the Louisiana National Guard, I'm used to handling weapons and I know New Orleans like the back of my hand..."

At that point, the telephone rang. Jonathan picked it up and very quickly handed it to me.

"It's for you," he said. Covering the receiver, he added: "I think it's Legendre."

I remembered that the Haitian had said he would call me back on Saturday morning.

"*Bonjour*, Monsieur Legendre," I said cautiously.

"Good morning, Professor Van Helsing," he replied. "Are you now ready *to exchange the keys*?"

"You're referring to the Key of Sakbata, I assume?"

"Of course. What else?"

"And in exchange for that Key, you would be willing to renounce all your claims on Saint-Amadou?"

"Precisely. I congratulate you for your accurate and succinct summary of my modest offer."

"Thank you," I said, insincerely. "There is, however, a difficulty."

"A difficulty?"

"Yes. And not a small one either. I have no idea where my uncle might have hidden the Key."

There was a silence on the line.

"That is rather problematic," he finally said.

"I think so too."

"I meant to say: it is rather problematic for you and the thousands of people who live in New Orleans."

"I don't understand," I lied.

He emitted a very unpleasant chuckle, a little like the cracking sound of bones breaking.

"You are trying to procrastinate in order to trick me, Professor."

I protested, rather uselessly.

"Not at all!"

"You have discovered that I own the Dagger of Hevioso. I used its power to divert Hurricane Katrina, which would otherwise have hit the Florida coast, towards New Orleans. It did occur to me that the last of the Van Helsings might very well, out of sheer stubbornness or foolish do-goodness, refuse to give me the Key of Sakbata, even at the cost of his beautiful house. But I'm reasonably certain that he will do so to save the lives of thousands of people, am I not correct?"

There was nothing to say. The bastard was indeed right, and he knew it.

"Katrina will hit New Orleans soon after midnight on Monday morning," he continued, "unless I use the

Dagger again to move the eye of the hurricane. My mobile is (504) 555-9922. You have until Sunday afternoon, a little more than 24 hours, to find the Key and give it to me; otherwise the destruction of New Orleans will become inevitable—and massive. Good-bye, Professor."

Click!

While I was on the phone, Jonathan had discreetly recorded our conversation and he and Zigor, with a set of headphones, had been able to listen in.

The young lawyer turned on the TV. It was just past 11 a.m. and the weathermen were predicting that Katrina would morph into a Category 4 hurricane, or possibly even a Category 5, during the night of Saturday to Sunday. Category 5 meant winds greater than 155 mph, roof failures, building collapsing, small houses being blown over, trees being blown down, cars and trucks being dragged through the streets, the complete destruction of mobile homes and major damage to the lower floors of all the structures located less than 15 feet above sea level and within 500 yards of the shoreline. In short: Hell on Earth.

Governor Blanco said she was going to ask President Bush to declare a Federal State of Emergency in the State of Louisiana. They also reported that the Mayor of New Orleans, the Honorable Ray Nagin, would give a press conference later in the day.

After listening to the avalanche of bad news, the three of us were pale as ghosts.

"We're in deep do-do," said Zigor.

"It's impossible," said Jonathan. "I don't believe it. A human being can't simply command the elements. It's... absurd!"

"Why not? Voodoo is one of Mankind's oldest religions. You could look at it this way: the Gods of its pantheon may only be the anthropomorphic representations of forces and energies that are already present in Nature, and which the so-called primitive peoples learned to control by creating archetypes like a 'God of Thunder,' etc. They are merely the psychological tools necessary to free certain powers that are inherent in the human mind, in order to accomplish what might seem to us to be miracles. In other words, you have to believe that you are a God in order to have the power of a God."

"You... you think so?" he asked, looking a little more confident.

"No," I replied with brutal honesty. "I gave you that speech because experience has taught me that it's the one that best reassures skeptics like you. But if you're going to join us in our mission, you'd better not feel too reassured..."

"You mean...?"

"Yes. Forget everything I just told you. The Gods do exist and they are evil."

He seemed shell-shocked. I thought it would take him a little while to digest it all. But if he insisted on joining our little combo after that, then at least he wouldn't be able to say that we hadn't warned him. Being a friend or an associate of a Van Helsing can be hazardous to one's health.

"If we could find the Key, we could set a trap for Legendre," suggested Zigor, who was chewing madly on his lower lip.

"Yes, but how do we find it?"

"Any clues, if there are any, must be at Saint-Amadou."

I agreed with him. There were no other possibilities. Uncle Ohisver must have left a note, or an indication somewhere: a safety deposit box in a bank, a crate buried in the garden; a loose floorboard in the attic... something... anything. He wasn't the kind of person to not take precautions.

"I'll come with you," said Jonathan, who now appeared to have come to terms with my revelations. "Three will speed up the search. I can't think of a better way to honor my father's memory."

I accepted his offer and, after closing up shop, we relocated to Saint-Amadou.

In movies, it is easy to suggest long, tiresome hours spent in research by a montage of quick edits. It only takes a couple of minutes and, with some nice music playing in the background, it is never boring. Reality is, sadly, starkly different.

Zigor, Jonathan and I, ably assisted by Zaka who was kept busy carrying boxes of documents containing family archives up and down the stairs, spent the entire afternoon poring over the paperwork accumulated by Uncle Ohisver during his entire life.

A life of adventure and feats of derring-do, which, at the end of the day, was more-or-less neatly filed away in the space of two dozen archival boxes filled with yellowed documents. Vanity of vanities, all is vanity... It was the study of all those papers and old letters that made me conscious, perhaps for the first time, that Uncle Ohisver was really and truly gone. Those mute testimonies to times long past were like the echoes of voices in an empty house.

At 5 p.m., Mayor Nagin gave his press conference. He proclaimed a State of Emergency and called for a voluntary evacuation of the city.

As the day outside grew ever darker, so did the atmosphere inside the House. We were rushing against the clock to find a clue, any clue that would enable us to locate the Key and perhaps stave off the apocalypse. We knew that if Katrina hit New Orleans at its maximum speed and power, little of the city would remain in its wake. It almost defied comprehension.

Two hours later, we still hadn't found anything. No mention anywhere of the Key of Sakbata or any other key for that matter. Yet, I knew Uncle Ohisver. He was a careful man; he wouldn't have entrusted the location of such a precious talisman to blind luck.

The secret had to be here, somewhere on this desk.

I ran again through the stash of notebooks collected by my ancestors. I found a detailed account of the battle that pit Ithamar Van Helsing against Phineas T. Barnum when the latter produced his Greatest Show on Earth in New Orleans on January 2, 1841. I read the true story of the *coup d'état* organized by Aharon Van Helsing against Haitian President Michel Domingue and his henchman Mayes, an evil Englishman who had become a *houngan* and who had owned the Key. I discovered the love letters written by Malachi Van Helsing to Josephine Balsamo after her stay at the House in 1900...

Those last two documents especially confirmed what Marie Laveau had told me about the four talismans; there was even an engraving of them dating back to Haiti's Napoleonic period.

I recognized the Dagger of Hevioso with its peculiar ebony handle, which I had seen in Legendre's hands.

The Medallion of Damballah was a small copper amulet with the image of the Serpent-God engraved on it. The Key of Sakbata looked to be an actual, small, key-like object with weirdly shaped teeth on its shaft, and made of some kind of dark wood. And the Cup of Erzulie was a silver goblet which...

Suddenly, I recognized that goblet!

It was the very same cup from which Marie Laveau had been drinking her mint julep!

So Marie was the owner of the Cup of Erzulie! Come to think of it, it wasn't too surprising, considering her position as Voodoo Queen.

"Come and look at this," I said.

Zigor stopped reading a biography of the sinister Rodil Mocquino, who had fought Ruven Van Helsing for possession of Saint-Amadou, and, followed by Jonathan, joined me. His trained eye immediately caught the similarities.

"It's Marie Laveau's cup!" he exclaimed.

"Uh huh," I said, while dialing the number for the Bienville Street store on the phone.

No one picked up the call.

"I've got to go," I said, finally. "We can't take the risk that Legendre might get his hands on a second talisman."

"Marie seems like she's pretty much able to take care of herself," remarked Zigor.

"If she didn't think it wise to tell you that she owned the Cup, perhaps you shouldn't..." added Jonathan.

"No," I replied, firmly. "I think that if Legendre gave us that extra day to find the Key, it was because he knew that the Cup was in New Orleans, too, and that he wanted to have the time to steal it, taking advantage of the disturbance caused by the hurricane and the evacuation. At the very least, I have to warn Marie. I agree that she can take care of herself, but Legendre isn't someone to sneeze at either. I'm positive he has a plan... I'll go to the shop, while you two stay here and continue the search without me."

"Are you sure this is a good idea?" asked Zigor.

"I won't go alone. Zaka will come with me."

The old man nodded his head enthusiastically. It must have reminded him of one of his crazy adventures with my uncle.

I walked towards the door.

"Wait, M'sieur Hugo," he said.

He rummaged through a drawer and pulled out an old 8mm 1892 ordnance revolver, of the type used by the French in Viet-Nam. He checked that the gun was loaded and in proper working order with a dexterity and professionalism that surprised even me. I knew that Uncle Ohisver and Zaka had been through some rough patches in their lives, but was more than a little disconcerting to see the naked proof of it displayed under my very eyes.

I asked the old man:

"Is *she* still in the garage?"

"Oh yes. M'sieur Ohisver was still taking her out for a ride every Sunday," he replied proudly.

We went out.

Night had fallen and the wind was rising as we went out to the garage attached at the left side of the house. The double doors were padlocked but Zaka had the key, which he pulled from one of the gold chains around his neck. We opened the doors without a hitch.

Inside was a jewel of a motorcar, one that Uncle Ohisver had loaned me all too infrequently, in my humble opinion, when I was a teenager. *She* was a real babe magnet that had never failed to provide me with attractive female company to cruise with in the French Quarter.

She was a '68 Dodge Charger, black, sleek and powerful. Steve McQueen drove one just like it in *Bullitt*. You would have to be made of stone to not succumb to her charms.

I sat behind the wheel. The keys were already in the ignition. The engine roared to life, purring like a big jungle cat which, at his master's command, could turn into a mean, mauling machine.

We drove slowly along St. Charles, towards the French Quarter. The night was oppressive and wet; the edge of the storm had reached us and it was pouring buckets.

The traffic had become extremely hazardous, murderous even. The locals hadn't waited for the evacuation orders; many had piled their belongings into pick-up trucks, trailers or the trunks of their cars, which were overflowing to the point of being held together with bungee cords and duct tape, and had begun to flee the city, driving like maniacs to escape the hurricane.

As they all had decided to leave at the same time, massive traffic pile-ups had begun, especially since no one seemed to have been in charge of telling the people which itineraries they were supposed to take. The city officials hadn't even thought of closing the inbound freeway lanes. I hated to think of the length of the traffic jams and all the people stuck there on their long voyages to nowhere.

We finally made it to Bienville in just under an hour. The revelers were few and far between in the French Quarter. Either tradition had gone out the window, or people were taking the threat of Katrina seriously indeed.

I parked the car just in front of the shop and immediately noticed a bad thing: the door was wide open, clearly the victim of a break-in.

I took a flashlight from the glove compartment and we got out of the car.

I entered the shop carefully; Zaka was covering me with his revolver.

Inside, it looked like a battlefield. Everything that could be broken, stomped, or trampled had been utterly destroyed. Katrina itself could not have been more destructive.

I tried the light switch, but there was no power.

I used my torch to look around. Towards the back of the store, lying crumpled on the floor, I saw a shape that I recognized immediately: a human body.

Zaka and I rushed towards the victim, who had bled profusely. The body was surrounded by a large pool of dark, viscous blood; Gaston had gone to meet his maker, after having been savagely struck multiple times by what looked like machete blows. The blood loss had done him in.

Zaka began praying for the poor man's soul. I interrupted him:

"Call 911, but first, give me your gun."

The old man complied. I felt more comfortable with the heavy revolver in my hand. The metallic smell of Gaston's blood turned up my stomach. Poor Gaston; luck hadn't been on his side.

I used the light to cautiously explore the rest of the shop, then began moving towards the back.

Suddenly, I heard repeated banging noises and a woman's scream.

I rushed towards the backroom, gun drawn, and discovered that the origin of the disturbance was a small adjacent kitchen, which led to an inside courtyard where the residents stored their grey trashcans.

I almost didn't need the light of my torch to see the two bulky silhouettes that were pummeling a walk-in pantry. The screams came from inside it.

One of the two men turned round to face me. He was enormous, clutching a machete, still dripping blood, in his hand. It was terrifyingly obvious who had killed Gaston.

"Who are you?" he asked.

From his accent, I deduced that he came from Haiti and, noting the savagery of his expression and the way he held his *coupe-chou*, I guessed that he had been at the notoriously sinister school of the Tontons Macoutes.

I pointed my gun at them, trying to sound as tough as possible.

"Stop!" I said. "One more step and you'll..."

Before I had time to finish my sentence, I heard a knife whistling towards me; the second man had thrown it. He had abandoned the idea of trying to get into the pantry and was advancing towards me.

I leaned to the side to avoid the blade and shot.

I hit the first Macoute in the shoulder. It wasn't a great shot. I needed more practice, as Farimba, one of my Hunters, kept telling me *ad nauseam*. I reflected that that shortcoming might cost me dearly.

The second Macoute was now upon me. Meanwhile, his pal was clutching his wounded shoulder, trying to staunch the blood, uttering horrible swear words in a Creole that I had never heard before.

I swung my heavy gun and used it as a truncheon to deliver a powerful blow to the head of my attacker, the type of blow that makes the ladies say later, "he was handsome... *before*"—even though in his case, I doubted it would make much of a difference. Blood started flowing from his skull and his nose and fell into his eyes, blinding him temporarily. I seized the opportunity to swiftly kick him where it would hurt the most. He immediately folded in half, then collapsed onto the floor, screaming and rolling around without any dignity whatsoever.

Meanwhile, the other Macoute seemed to be feeling better, or angrier, and was trying to reduce my height by a head with a swing of his machete. In a confined space like the kitchenette, I didn't have as much room as I would have liked to avoid his reach. But I had learned the art of *capoeira* in Brazil. It's a form of unarmed combat that 16th century slaves used to protect themselves. A swift *banda* to the legs later, and he too was sprawled on the floor without having had time to understand where the blow that had laid him out had come from. I grabbed the machete out of his hand, breaking his wrist with my heel in the process, then used the flat of its blade to conk him on the head and send him straight into the Sandman's arms.

Zaka returned just as I was opening the pantry to let out Ascension, who had locked herself inside. I instructed my old friend to tie the two Macoutes securely.

"It's over," I told the red-haired girl. "You have nothing to fear."

"Professor Van Helsing..."

"Please call me Hugo."

78

"...You saved my life. Those pigs killed Gaston and..."

Just to be safe, I asked:

"How many were they?"

"Five," she replied, without thinking. Then, as she saw the two bodies on the floor, realization dawned and her eyes grew wider.

"Oya!" she exclaimed.

"Marie!" I said.

I immediately rushed into the tunnel that led to the Voodoo Queen's courtyard. I noticed that Ascension was right behind me.

"You don't think you've had enough fear and loathing for the evening?" I said.

"I can't abandon her," she said.

We didn't have time for an argument which I knew I would lose anyway, so I gave her the machete I had taken from the Macoute.

"Use the pointy bit," I advised.

"Thank you," she said.

We came out onto the patio where Marie usually held court and I noticed right away that she hadn't just happened to be called Voodoo Queen for nothing.

Three bodies were stretched out on the tiles. Ascension couldn't keep from looking away. I wished I could have done it too, because the images of those three bloody corpses that looked exactly as if a giant hand had squeezed them, causing all their insides to burst out of their flesh, was going to haunt my nights for many years to come.

Marie, on the other hand, was gone. There was no trace of her—or of the silver goblet which was the Cup of Erzulie. Legendre had failed.

Marie seems like she's pretty much able to take care of herself, Zigor had said earlier.

He'd hit the nail on the head.

We stayed to take care of the formalities after the police finally arrived. Soon after, two ambulances left, one with Gaston's body, the other with the two Macoutes. Ascension told the cops that two junkies had tried to rob the store and rape her, not necessarily in that order, and her loyal cousin, visiting Professor Van Helsing, had miraculously dropped by and done his duty as a Good Samaritan.

Ordinarily, an incident like that would have warranted only a half-hearted investigation anyway, but on a night like that, with Katrina and the evacuation of the city, the police had a lot of bigger fish to fry than to worry about the fate of two junkies.

All's well that ends well would likely be the conclusion of their brief report.

It was about 11 p.m. when we found ourselves standing on the curb outside, alone at last.

"We can't leave the store open like that," I told Ascension. "Anyone could just walk in and I have a feeling there are some people who'll be just too happy to take advantage of the storm to start looting anything they can carry."

"They broke the door; it won't shut," she said.

"We'll use some plywood; that'll secure it from the hurricane too. I saw some on the corner. Zaka, could you go and grab me a sheet? It'll only take a minute."

Waiting for the old man to return, I looked at the lock. It was a magnetic lock, of the type that uses a card-key and a combination.

"Do you have the key?" I asked Ascension.

And suddenly, an idea came to me, without warning, in fact, it was a bit like an epiphany...

We drove back to Saint-Amadou slowly and carefully in the dismal night, plowing our way through the whipping rain and the furious wind.

While Zaka parked the car, I ushered Ascension into the House. And then, I discovered that the terrors of the night had only begun.

Two bodies were on the floor of the library in a pool of blood: Jonathan, with a nasty-looking knife planted in his back, and my friend Zigor, my comrade and trusted ally, almost entirely decapitated.

Sunday, August 28

I'M READY TO REOPEN NEGOTIATIONS.

Zigor was dead.

I just couldn't get used to the thought. It was long past 1 a.m. and none of us had been able to fall asleep.

I kept replaying images of my past adventures with the ex-hippie lawyer in my mind: at LAX, after our battle with Dracula... in New York, at the Amsterdammer Club, where Zigor slurped through soda cans with the discretion of a roto-rooter... in Washington, where he saved my life when he pulled me out of the *reflection* of the Lincoln Memorial...

I could still see him, chewing carefully on one of his ketchup-dripping veggie burgers while listening to tapes of Joe Dassin... coming up with amazingly devious schemes to outwit the legal sharks of Morrison, Morrison & Dodd... Zigor, Zigor, where are you now?

I wasn't the type to drown my sorrows in booze, nor to put my fist through a wall. So I did what we Van Helsings do best: repress, bury our emotions and get back to work.

I had told Zaka to put the body in our cold storage room. I felt we would have plenty of time to deal with formalities later, and that it might abuse the good will of the local boys in blue to call them twice in the same night. I didn't think that any of Zigor's five ex-wives would be in a particular rush to learn of their ex's demise. The tears and the gnashing of teeth would come later, at the opening of the will, when they would discover that he had bequeathed his not inconsiderable fortune in equal halves to the Club and to Joe Dassin's fan club.

Jonathan eventually told us what had happened after Zaka had patched him up. The young attorney wasn't dead, as we had at first thought. The knife had missed any major arteries or organs and, other than the shock to his system and the blood loss, he was generally OK. Zaka made him drink some awful Cajun concoction which soon had him back on his feet, although his face remained a slightly greenish color for several hours afterwards.

As he explained it, Zigor was doing some research on the Internet... He couldn't tell us what exactly, and a quick look at the portable didn't show us anything immediately useful... There was one e-mail from Citrin regarding real estate leases, but nothing else. Jonathan was reading through my uncle's early diaries, from when he had gone gallivanting around South America with Che Guevara; nothing there, either. He probably hadn't even heard of the Key of Sakbata at the time.

Then, suddenly, four Tontons Macoutes had burst into the House and attacked them. We saw the results when we arrived. When Legendre struck, he did it with the Powell doctrine of using overwhelming force.

Jonathan wanted to call the police, but I swiftly talked him out of it after detailing what had happened at Marie Laveau's shop earlier. We both agreed that we didn't have time to deal with the authorities just then.

Katrina was almost upon us. CNN had just given us another news update, confirming that the hurricane had indeed reached Category 4. The experts thought it would soon reach Category 5. That was grim news. A tactical nuclear device might prove less devastating than what was in store for us. And we were right at the center of all of it.

And Zigor was dead. Perhaps he was the lucky one after all.

The aftershock of the night's traumatic events was starting to weigh heavily on me. I felt myself rambling, losing the thread... I knew that I had had a brilliant idea just outside of Marie's shop earlier, but now I couldn't remember what it was. It was something about a clue that might lead us to the location of the Key... But no matter how hard I tried to focus, it kept evading me. I couldn't concentrate. I needed to shut my eyes and tune out.

I told Zaka to put Ascension in Zigor's room and Jonathan in Uncle Ohisver's and I went to bed.

I knew where the Key was.

I woke up with a start and a remarkably clear and restored mind. Sleep had again worked its magic.

The clock said it was just after 6:30 a.m. Normally it should have been dawn, except that it was still dark outside.

I took a quick shower, got dressed and rushed down to the library. I now remembered what had caught my attention the night before.

Looking at Ascension's magnetic key card had reminded me that, in my uncle's wallet, I had found a hotel bill, folded in three around another magnetic key card, of the type most hotels use these days.

It was a key, not of the conventional type perhaps, but a key nevertheless.

And it was possibly also the clue we had been seeking!

At 7 a.m., Zaka showed up and started to make coffee. I turned on the news. As we expected, Katrina was now officially a Category 5 hurricane.

I had found the hotel bill and the key card on the desk, just where I had left them. The hotel was the Charlevoix, located on St. Louis. The bill was for two nights during Mardi-Gras. The key card was indeed just like Ascension's, the same model used by millions of other stores and hotels throughout America; nothing extraordinary about it.

The bill identified the room as 278. It was an apocalyptic number, but I doubted that mattered. Uncle Ohisver wasn't particularly fond of math and number games.

I had grabbed the telephone when Ascension and Jonathan arrived, soon followed by Zaka and a pot of steaming coffee.

"I think I may have hit upon the answer," I explained, while we each shared a cup.

"Do you think Mr. Van Helsing hid the Key in that hotel room?" asked Jonathan.

"Perhaps not, but at the very least, he might have left another clue there," I said, while dialing the Charlevoix on the phone.

When they answered, I asked for room 278. That's when, my beautiful, sparkling brand-new theory completely collapsed, deader than dead, at my feet. There was no room 278.

"I don't get it," said Jonathan.

"Just another wild goose chase," muttered Ascension, looking discouraged.

Unlike what usually happens in films or TV series, I didn't have another epiphany. After such high hopes, the sense of disappointment was even more painful. We just kept thinking, mulling the facts over and over in our heads, but producing no new theories, no new solutions.

Was the card key a clue left by Uncle Ohisver, or had I been wrong from the start?

I couldn't believe it. All my instincts told me that I was close to the answer. It was within my grasp. If only I could figure it out...

We decided to continue our search and dig deeper into my uncle's papers, looking for some kind of connection we might have missed the first time.

Two hours later, we still hadn't made any progress. It was now 9 a.m. and Mayor Nagin had just issued the first ever mandatory evacuation order of New Orleans.

"That's going to complicate matters," said Jonathan.

"Why?" I said. "We have no choice but to ignore it. You can go if you want."

"No, of course not, I'll stay with you."

"I'd like to find Oya," said Ascension, "but I don't know where she is."

"I'm pretty sure that if she required your presence," I said, "she'd send for you. I think she's keeping you away for your own safety."

"But she might be in danger."

"She almost certainly *is* in danger, but you saw last night that she's perfectly capable of taking care of herself. Besides, I have a good idea of where she might be hiding, and if I'm right, it'll take Legendre a lot more than a bunch of Tontons Macoutes to dislodge her."

"What? You know the location of her sacred *houn-for*?" said Ascension with a tinge of envy in her voice.

"Don't get cross, Ascension. Marie has known my family since she taught the Voodoo rites to Yakob Van

Helsing in the 18th century. She and the Van Helsings go way back, as they say. We're sort of bound at the hip."

"If I follow what you're saying," said Jonathan, "this Marie Laveau character has more hideaways than a Texas outlaw. In fact, the only place she doesn't seem to be is her tomb."

I would have smiled at Jonathan's little quip if I had had the energy. He was, of course, referring to Marie's so-called tomb, which is in fact that of her daughter, Marie Glapion, who used to impersonate her mother in the 19th century. It is one of New Orleans' most famous tourist landmarks, and, like Jim Morrison's grave at the Père Lachaise cemetery in Paris, it's been defiled with graffiti. While the faithful, the pilgrims, the desperate and the kooks keep leaving flowers on it. They say that if you draw a cross on the tomb and knock three times, Marie will grant you a wish. Really!

But Jonathan's casual gibe suddenly sparked an idea. I knew that Marie's tomb was located in New Orleans' St. Louis Cemetery No. 1, the city's oldest graveyard, built in 1789. The Hotel Charlevoix, too, was on St. Louis, quite close to the Cemetery, in fact. Could there be a connection between the two?

"I need a map," I said.

"What kind of map?" asked Ascension.

"A map of Cemetery No. 1."

"I think I saw one in the library," said Jonathan.

"Get it! And hurry!"

I unfolded the map on the desk. It was relatively recent, having been put together with information from the Archdiocesan Cemeteries, City Commission and the 2001 Survey Project. Each tomb was numbered.

Tomb 278 was located just near St. Louis at the very end of Alley 8-R.

"Whose tomb is this?" asked Jonathan.

"No one," said Ascension, who was looking at the database. "The name is blank."

"It belongs to my family," I said.

"What?"

"The first occupant of tomb 278 was Talia Van Helsing, who died during the Battle of New Orleans in 1815. It's her son, Ithamar, who built Saint-Amadou. For reasons of, shall we say, security, we, Van Helsings, have always thought it wise to hide the places where we bury our own. We have a vault under the Amsterdammer Club in New York and another one in Prague. That's where Uncle Ohisver hid the Key of Sakbata. And that's why only a Van Helsing could solve this mystery."

Eventually noon arrived, but you wouldn't have known it from the dismal quality of light. The sky was the color of lead as the hurricane crept ever closer. The whipping rain and the wind constantly battered at the House and we huddled inside to avoid the fury of the elements.

While eating sandwiches and listening to the news on WWL-TV, we learned that not everyone had been either able or willing to leave New Orleans. The Mayor had established several "refuges of last resort" for those citizens who could not leave, including the Louisiana Superdome, which could shelter approximately 26,000 people. In my opinion, it wouldn't be enough. I also wondered how they planned to provide all those people with enough food and water to last for several days once the storm came ashore... It didn't look good.

Despite pleas for help, the Federal Government seemed as reactive as a dead possum in the middle of the road. There were no bus convoys to help with the evacuation, no National Guard either, most of them being already deployed in Iraq. One million people had reportedly fled the city, but many had found themselves stuck on highways that were so jammed up it was impossible to go anywhere. One reporter said that the *USS Bataan* was moored in the Gulf of Mexico, approximately 100 miles south of New Orleans, but wasn't doing anything, awaiting God knows what orders!

New Orleans was little more than a panicked prey, paralyzed by fear, standing helpless and trembling in the sights of a hunter it knew it couldn't escape.

But I didn't have time to reflect on the presumed incompetence or venality of the various spheres of the American government. There was still a chance to avoid the worst, if we could force Legendre, by hook or by crook, to divert the eye of the hurricane once again.

It was up to us to head out and brave the elements to find the Key of Sakbata, but this time, we planned to do it adequately prepared.

"Zaka," I said.

"Yes, M'sieur Hugo?"

"I saw some crates in the cellars labeled *Nicaragua*. Are they...?"

Zaka nodded, knowing what I meant.

"Take what you think we'll need," I instructed. "I trust you."

Ascension and Jonathan looked at me, vaguely puzzled, but I didn't think it was necessary to explain to them that, sometime during the 1980s, Uncle Ohisver had been running guns for the Sandinistas, and that he had kept several "free samples" in his cellar.

Zaka returned with four Portuguese AR-10s, the belt-fed type. Good old Sandinistas! It's the little gifts that keep friendship warm, they say.

After loading two boxes of ammo in the trunk of the Dodge, we hit the road.

The winds had already reached 50 mph and the speed continued to ramp up. I was worried we wouldn't be able to drive at all, and although that didn't prove to be the case, we were forced to go at a painstakingly slow crawl to get through the rain squalls and the debris that whipped everywhere around us; the headlights barely pierced the pervasive gloom.

From time to time, I saw city buses filled with residents they'd gathered from various pickup points throughout the city and shuttling them to the so-called "shelters of last resort." They looked like the Flying Dutchman, endlessly battling the storm, having just traded his soul to the Devil for an everlasting journey across the infinite seas. Where would they end up? Would they make it through the hurricane? What would be their ultimate fates? I didn't dare think of the answers to those questions.

Virtually deserted, abandoned by most of its inhabitants, New Orleans was left to fend for itself. There was a smell in the air which I recognized from my trips to Kosovo, Rwanda and Kazakhstan. It was the stench of the Beast, the stink of chaos and rot, of forsaking all standards of human decency and dignity... That odor floated upon the city like a shroud covering a corpse. Even the French Quarter, which had a long tradition of giving the finger to hurricanes with all night partying in a symbolic gesture of defiance, seemed strangely silent.

The journey reminded me of driving over the mountains of Burma during a monsoon, and it was just as enjoyable. Finally, we arrived at the gates of Cemetery No. 1; I parked the Dodge just outside. I didn't think we had to worry about the parking goons impounding it.

I took a crowbar and a few "accessories" from the trunk. With the AR-10s thrown over our shoulders, we didn't look like the faithful coming to say a prayer at the tomb of any dearly departed, instead, we resembled debt collectors from the Tijuana cartel.

The entrance to the Cemetery still featured the same plaque from the Archdiocese warning that "visitors enter these premises at their own risk" and that they "disclaim all responsibilities for their personal safety." One wonders what on Earth the Archdiocese knows—and the public doesn't—about what truly goes on in that cemetery that they feel the need to cover their Ecclesiastical asses with such a dire warning.

We quickly passed by Marie Laveau's tomb, or rather Marie Glapion's, with its pitiful graffiti begging for some favor from beyond the grave; its flower pots lay shattered by the violence of the storm. I didn't think it was a particularly auspicious beginning.

Finally, we arrived at Tomb 278, a sad and forlorn grave, long abandoned, located at the very end of alley 8-R, just against the wall of St. Louis. It bore no name, no markings and there were no flowers to serve as decoration. There was simply an anonymous marble slate next to a modest mausoleum of grey stucco: *Vanitas Vanitatum, Omnia Vanitas.* I was reminded of a poem by Anne Brontë:

In all we do, and hear, and see,
Is restless Toil, and Vanity.

While yet the rolling Earth abides,
Men come and go like ocean tides;

And ere one generation dies,
Another in its place shall rise;
That, sinking soon into the grave,
Others succeed, like wave on wave.

With her mother taken by cancer, and herself and her two sisters plagued by pulmonary tuberculosis, a disease which killed her at age 29, Anne had quickly been forced to master the essential fact of life that was, primarily, how to deal with death. She understood that through death, we seek eternal renewal and redemption, and that may well be the overwhelming strength of our species.

I decided it wasn't really the time to dwell on such morbid thoughts (no matter how philosophically interesting they were) and instead used the crowbar to force open the mausoleum. In less than a minute, I had destroyed the lock, which was neither old nor rusted; another fact that lent credence to my theory.

I pushed open the small grille, which fell to the ground with a clang that was loud enough to be heard over the howling of the gale. Inside were two small marble shelves, normally meant for ex-votos. They were empty, except for an object made of dark wood with unusually shaped teeth on its shaft and a round, jagged head. It fit the description in the memoirs of Malachi Van Helsing like, well, like a key.

And, indeed, it was the Key of Sakbata.

I grabbed it and immediately noticed that it was oddly warm to my touch. Then, I began to experience a series of strange sensations. Peculiar sounds, smells and colors normally invisible to an ordinary man began to filter around the edges of my perception. I heard *slithy* sounds, saw *tovey* shades... The line of Lewis Carroll's poem drifted unbidden into my mind: *Beware the Jubjub bird and shun the frumious Bandersnatch...*

"Watch out! Get down!" I suddenly shouted.

Through my strange, new senses, I had perceived the presence of dark, ominous figures slinking between the tombs. Holding the Key made me more aware of my surroundings, in a vivid, almost surreally clear fashion.

We were lucky, because four gunshots immediately rang out. I heard the bullets whiz by. We would have all been dead if I hadn't warned my companions.

It was Legendre's Tontons Macoutes!

We began running like madmen through the macabre maze of tombs and alleys that was St. Louis Cemetery No. 1, playing some sinister but deadly game of hide-and-seek with our pursuers. Because of the storm, it was neither light nor dark; we were trapped between night and day, in a kind of perpetual twilight.

Zaka hadn't waited for my instructions to fire back. The old man had shot off two rounds, which had killed two of our opponents. I saw them drop between the cold marble of the tombs like flailing scarlet medusae, throbbing with reddish light before slowly growing dim, then dark.

Zaka was moving between the tombs with surprising agility for a man of his age. Even the collection of holy medals hanging around his neck seemed more silent than usual. Between two rounds of gunfire, he prayed for the souls of the men he had just killed. If that worked for him, who was I to criticize?

Ascension and Jonathan struggled with their guns, trying to hold their own, but they just didn't have my experience, or Zaka's. Fortunately, they were able to find shelter behind the mausoleums.

I quickly came to the conclusion that Legendre's Macoutes were drugged to the gills. They barely seemed to feel pain when hit by our bullets, and even with blood gushing from their wounds, they still found the strength to leap over the graves or climb on them like mad monkeys. They were everywhere.

We had the superior weapons, but they way outnumbered us. As we ran by, they tried to grab us with claws; they all sported specially-filed, pointy, razor-sharp fingernails, When they missed, the deadly, whistling sound of their machetes slicing through the air buzzed by our ears. There were far too many near-misses for my taste.

We were drenched from head to toes; the rain fell in sheets, flowing into our eyes, and making it even more difficult to see where we were going. We were out of breath and out of time.

Zaka was the first to fall. I stopped to help him get back to his feet.

"Zaka!"

"M'sieur Hugo..."

"One last effort, old friend, we're almost there."

I wasn't lying. We had managed to circle around and were barely 500 yards from the exit, but standing between it and us were Legendre's blood-thirsty hordes and they had no intentions of letting us through.

Alone, I could have carried Zaka and forced my way through, but with Ascension and Jonathan in tow, I knew I would be toast.

I grabbed the Key and held it high up in the air.

"Legendre!" I shouted. "Call off your dogs or I'll destroy the Key!"

From somewhere within the Cemetery, strangely close and yet distant, I heard the evil *houngan* shout back. In fact, I wondered briefly if I wasn't the only one who heard him, through those strange new senses of mine that the ownership of the Key had conferred upon me.

"The Key is indestructible, Professor Van Helsing, you know that as well as I do," he cackled.

"The object itself, perhaps," I replied. "But its power can be nullified if I recite the Conjuration of Mawu-Lisa."

There was a very long silence, and I knew I had scored a point. A big one.

"You... You know the Conjuration of Mawu-Lisa? But only Great Initiates..." said Ascension, who seemed just as surprised as I imagined Legendre was.

"I'm a Van Helsing," I said, modestly. "It's part and parcel of our education."

"What the Hell are you two talking about?" asked Jonathan, who couldn't contain his irritation.

"Mawu-Lisa is the supreme Godhead of the Voo-doo," I explained. "A cosmic male-female duality. Only they can remove the power of the talismans—if they want to."

"Would they?"

Ah-ha! I thought. Jonathan the skeptic appeared to have taken a hike, leaving a new, believing Jonathan in his place.

"Maybe, if I ask them nicely," I replied. "But I don't think that's a chance Legendre is ready to take."

I was right, because suddenly, I heard his voice carried on the wings of the storm.

"Professor Van Helsing!"

"Monsieur Legendre."

"It seems that I underestimated you."

"We all make mistakes."

"I'm ready to reopen negotiations. What do you want?"

"I will surrender the Key on two conditions. The first, that we all leave this place safe and sound..."

"Of course."

"...and the second that you use the Dagger to call off the hurricane."

"That is now impossible. But I can weaken it and divert its course so that the eye will not hit New Orleans."

"Then do it and I'll leave the Key inside the tomb where we are now. As soon as we're out of here, you can come and get it. You have my word."

"Very well, I agree to your terms."

Legendre suddenly stepped out from behind another tomb. The elegant banker I had met earlier was gone, replaced by a frightful scarecrow of a man, dressed in tattered black clothes that looked like they had come straight from out of a grave. He was a terrifyingly sinister sight and I preferred to not know the origins of his macabre attire.

He held the Dagger of Hevioso high in his left hand.

In response, I showed him the Key, and then very slowly and visibly, I deposited it on a marble shelf inside the tomb that sheltered us. I gestured to show Legendre where it was.

"Now it's your turn!" I shouted.

The Haitian brandished the Dagger at the storm, made several gestures and uttered a few words which I couldn't hear.

There was a brief, supernatural flash of lightning. I figured it was only visible to those with magical perceptions, because while Ascension blinked, Jonathan didn't seem to notice.

"It is done," said Legendre.

"He's telling the truth," said Ascension.

"I think so too," I said.

Her powers as Marie Laveau's young apprentice enabled her to do simple readings of men's souls, and she knew Legendre was sincere. As for me, I had ranked among the top five players at the Texas Hold'em championship in Reno three years in a row when I was a student at USC.

We rushed towards the exit, guns in hand, looking behind us to make sure that Legendre's Tontons Macoutes weren't coming after us, but the Haitian appeared to be keeping his word.

We ran out of the Cemetery, dripping with water. Just as we got into the Dodge, I heard the sound of an explosion behind us.

I swiftly closed the passenger door behind Zaka, whom I had helped into the car, and jumped behind the wheel. We took off in a geyser of water and drove off as fast as we safely could.

Seeing Ascension and Jonathan's questioning looks in the rearview mirror, I felt I owed them an explanation.

"I pulled the pin from a grenade I left behind next to the Key. I'm hoping it took care of Legendre—but I'm not under any illusions..."

"What about the Conjuration of Mawu-Lisa?" asked Ascension with growing understanding in her eyes.

"Pure bluff."

It was in instances like this that I appreciated bearing the name of Van Helsing. People were all to willing to believe any of us could perform miracles; I could pretend I was the Anti-Pope Felix VI and there were those who would ask me for the Last Rites.

It was 7 p.m. by the time we got back to Saint-Amadou and the city was entirely swallowed up by the darkness.

I had known more than my fair share of hurricanes in New Orleans when I was a boy, but none of them had ever before succeeded in forcing Molly's at the Market to shut its doors. But of course, Katrina was no ordinary hurricane...

As we had driven past Molly's on Decatur, I saw the dark green shutters closed and the famous mustard yellow building locked up. The crowd which normally would have gathered there to drink all night and defy the fury of the storm with creole rum and hurricane punch had stayed home. The owner—I didn't know if it was still old Jim Monaghan, or his son—had wisely chosen caution over tradition. It's true that the notion of a bunch of drunken revelers cruising around the French Quarter in winds of over 100 mph wasn't confidence-inspiring.

Nearby, Café Lafitte was also closed. I guessed that its owner, Tip Andrews, and his two dogs, Gigi and Dijon, had vamoosed as well. There were still a few colored balloons, purple, green and gold, hanging sadly from the lampposts, mercilessly being ripped down by the winds. And like the balloons, the would-be carousers were gone as well, carried off by the storm or hiding somewhere in safety.

We were eager to follow suit.

*IT WOULD SEEM THAT THE SYMBOLISTS WERE
WRONG.*

Do I have to tell you that none of us slept much that night? While the hurricane raged on, we kept our eyes and ears glued to the TV and the radio.

Saint-Amadou was a well-built house, which had the added benefit of some, shall we say, "special" protections, and yet it was shaken like it was a rag doll. And the garden district was not nearly as badly hit as other sections of town.

At 6:10 a.m., Katrina made landfall near Buras-Triumph, Louisiana. By then, it had decreased to only a Category 3 hurricane—which still meant sustained winds of 125 mph. But Legendre had been true to his word and our last minute bargain had spared New Orleans the worst.

We were buffeted by eight to ten inches of torrential rains. The winds that ravaged the city uprooted trees, wrecked building, smashed windows and lifted cars as if they were Tonka Toys. The noise was appalling: it sounded like a jumbo jet was taking off in the street. Hundred-year-old trees simply folded over like so many blades of grass.

When we eventually decided it was safe to go out, around 9 a.m., the hurricane had passed. Surprisingly, the sun was shining. There was a strange odor in the air—ozone, perhaps? At last, we were able to assess the extent of the damage: there was debris everywhere, downed branches, overturned cars... Our old eucalyptus tree had survived this time; it lay on the street, partially uprooted. We had been lucky that it hadn't hit Saint-Amadou when it fell.

We thought that we—and New Orleans—had survived the worst. We were wrong, because the worst was still to come.

Before continuing with my narrative, I feel that I need to give a brief account of what was happening elsewhere in New Orleans, based on what I learned later on.

The true tragedy of Katrina wasn't caused by the Gods of the Voodoo, or even by the hurricane, but was a product of man's greed and foolishness.

As I noted earlier, the whole of New Orleans, squarely stuck between the Mississippi and Lake Pontchartrain, was, depending on the neighborhood, between 10 and 100 inches below sea level.

Over the years, and particularly since World War II, the U.S. Army Corps of Engineers had carried out various landmark projects along the Mississippi, changing the course of the river, clearing sand banks, draining swamps, building dykes, digging canals, all with the intent of reclaiming a maximum amount of usable land and thereby increasing the harbor's capacity. As a result, the ancient natural barriers that had protected the city for so long, like swamp lands, islets and sand banks, had been sacrificed on the altar of progress.

Furthermore, as was sadly all too often the case on major public works, it was later discovered that many shortcuts had been taken which had weakened the original plans. For example, there were foundations that were supposed to have been 18 feet deep but were only 10!

So, when an immense, moving wall of water, up to 20 feet high, began rushing upon the Parishes south and east of the city, the levees broke, the canals overflowed and the whole of New Orleans was soon underwater.

At 6:30 a.m., the waters of Lake Borgne, northeast of the city, began to flood St. Bernard Parish. Less than an hour later, all the eastern sections of the city, from Bywater to Mid-City were flooded; then, at 8 a.m., it was the Ninth Ward's turn. The waters overturned houses as if they were made of Lego bricks; in less than two hours, hundreds of residents who had managed to survive the wrath of the hurricane itself, were drowned like rats.

At 10 a.m., the canals of London Avenue and 17th Street gave up and the flood spread to the neighborhoods of Lakeview and Metairie. The garden district and the French Quarter were spared, but, at noon, 80% of New Orleans was underwater—in some places, by as much as 15 feet!

The sewers backed up; the refineries and the public landfills filled the water with the most toxic refuse imaginable, turning it into a noxious, foul-smelling soup that seeped everywhere and destroyed everything. The refugees who, by then, had climbed to the rooftops of their houses, or were adrift on makeshift boats, desperately looked for rescuers—but no one came.

New Orleans, abandoned by the Federal Government, was on its own. The city began to sink into a dark abyss, where the brief moment of hope that had succeeded the passing of the hurricane, was suddenly replaced by the darkest despair. Chaos erupted in places—although less than what was later reported on the news. Looting started in the areas that had been more or less spared by the flood. Meanwhile, inside the Superdome,

the refugees, haggard, exhausted, lacking food and water, looked for succor—none was to be found. People
died and their bodies were simply left where they were
or drifted away on the dark waters, a mute testimony to
the anarchy that had taken over the city.

Those are only a few of the darkest moments that
New Orleans experienced during the hellish days that it
suffered in Katrina's wake. As for us, after we had as-
sessed the damage to the House and the neighborhood,
we returned to Saint-Amadou, intent on planning our
next move.

Or at least, that's what we would have done if Zaka
hadn't made a horrifying discovery as soon as we returned. He had gone into the kitchen to check on the
food and saw that the cold room had been opened—from
the inside—and that Zigor's body was gone!

"That's impossible!" screamed Jonathan when he
heard the news.

He had to see for himself. He rushed into the
kitchen and quickly returned, his face a portrait of fear
and uncertainty. I knew that look well: it was the look of
someone who had seen a ghost, while refusing to believe
such things existed. Jonathan's entire mental foundations
had again been shaken to their core.

"It's not only possible," I said, "but entirely too
logical. Obviously, Legendre survived my grenade..."

"...And is using the Key to reanimate the dead and
turn them into zombies," finished Ascension. "It's monstrous."

"He now has two talismans: the Dagger of Hevioso
and the Key of Sakbata," I said. "No one knows what
happened to the Medallion of Damballah, but we do

know who has the Cup of Erzulie: Marie Laveau. My guess is that he's going after it."

"Do we know what he wants?" asked Jonathan.

"Not yet. But even if we did, would it change anything? I don't think so. We know what he's capable of, and we have no choice but to stop him."

"How? We're even more helpless than before," said Ascension.

"True. So, we'd better find Marie. She has the Cup, and the knowledge and power to use it. We know that, but so does Legendre, which I think is why he has gathered an army of zombies to help him in his confrontation with her. My guess is that we cost him more lives than we thought yesterday at the Cemetery."

"Maybe," said Jonathan, "but we don't know where Marie is hiding."

Ascension looked at me. Her curiosity slowly changed into a growing awareness that *someone* actually knew where Marie was. Me.

When she looked like that, capable of great intuitive leaps—and more—she reminded me of her grandmother, Carême Proudfoot, who was Ruven Van Helsing's mistress. We were cousins, of sorts, and the Van Helsing gene was clearly manifest in her. I didn't like to betray Marie's secrets, but, under the circumstances, I didn't think I had a choice.

"Marie owns a mansion in the old section of Bayou St. John," I explained. "That's where she used to live in the 18th century under the name of Sanité Dédé. That was the *hounfor* where she initiated Talia Van Helsing who, in 1872, at age 21 and with Marie's help, repelled the *Boum'ba Maza*, the entities responsible for the Great Fire of New Orleans. In an emergency, I'm sure that is the one place where she would seek refuge."

"But Bayou St. John is already underwater," exclaimed Jonathan, who had been keeping track of the floods on TV.

It suddenly dawned on me that Armageddon, if and when it came, would be televised 24/7 on CNN. I couldn't wait.

My watch showed it was 7 p.m. when we arrived at Bayou St. John.

It had taken us nearly all day to find a flat-bottomed boat, or *chaland*, as the old Cajuns called them, of the type that had been in use in Louisiana since the early colonial days. With its blunt bow and stern, it was extremely stable and well-suited to Louisiana's swamps. It had been stored in a forgotten corner of Saint-Amadou's cellars, behind an old armoire. Only Zaka remembered we had one. We had to fix it up before we used it though, because it was in a rather sorry state, not having been used for probably 20 years. The wood was rotten in places, but nothing that a bit of do-it-yourself carpentry couldn't take care of.

Once we'd done that, we had tied the boat to the top of the Dodge with rope. All that had taken a huge amount of time and effort, but even though we were dirty and sweaty, we nevertheless felt exhilarated when we finally reached our goal.

Bayou St. John is one of New Orleans' most remarkable historical neighborhoods. It' s crossed by canals that are bordered by superb colonial-style mansions. Its name comes from Fort Saint-Jean, which the French had erected on its location at the beginning of the 18th century. The natives, who had been here long before the Gallic invaders, called it *Bayouk Choupic*, when it was still only a putrid swamp connecting Lake Pontchartrain to the Mississippi. They crossed it on small canoes and tended to died young, either taken by disease or eaten by the mephitic wild life that thrived there.

I reflected that History must love irony, because Katrina had sent Bayou St. John racing back to its roots: it was, once again, a rotten swamp upon which one crossed in a small boat, risking one's life at each and every turn.

The water was waist-high; it was dark, dirty and fetid, polluted by the sewers, stinking of gasoline and excrement. The few residents who had survived the storm had long fled—at least, those who were able to get hold of boats like ours. As for the others... It wasn't too hard to imagine their fates and the thought of it turned my stomach. All around us, attics were filled with the bodies of the trapped; they had already started to decompose and the smell had begun to attract scavengers...

I was using a pole to propel our boat forward, just as I used to do when I was a student in Cambridge. Several times I had felt it brush against nameless things that slithered silently in the dark waters. I thought they were alligators, or perhaps water snakes that had left their usual haunts to come and partake in this unusual and ignoble feast.

The modern city that I knew had been all but eradicated and replaced by a savage jungle; where civilization had once stood, wilderness once again reigned. It was unthinkable that the putrid swamp that held the rotting bodies of American citizens, had, only a few days before, been part of one of the most beautiful cities of the United States—a city where the beasts of the bayous suddenly had license to prowl and feast on the corpses of its residents.

I guided our boat safely through the watery maze and the encroaching darkness because I had been here before, a long time ago, under very different circumstances...

Uncle Ohisver had wanted to personally introduce me to Marie Laveau. I was only eight or nine at the time. He had told me that she was an old family friend, a fact which hadn't particularly surprised me because I had already come to the realization that our family had many *old friends* around the world...

I still remembered our first meeting. Marie had laid out the small ebony tray, the ivory prayer beads, the 36 palm nuts and the other sacred tools used by the *bokonon*, the seers of the Voodoo, whose rituals date back to the oldest African antiquity. I studied the Art later on, but I can't reveal its secrets. What Marie read of my destiny that day, neither Ohisver nor I ever learned. But since then, I was forever in her eyes a *vodunsi*, an adept of the *Vodun*, or Voodoo, even though I never fully subscribed to her religion.

Later, at Cap-Haitien, where my family still owns the estate that Raziel Van Helsing acquired in the 17th century, I met the great *houngan* Soulagé Minfort, who taught me the arts of the *bokonon*. He, too, immediately accepted me as a *vodunsi*, marked from birth, according to him, by the Gods themselves.

All those memories came unbidden to my mind as I steered our boat towards Marie Laveau's last refuge, advancing slowly upon the dark waters filled with nameless horrors.

Zaka, Ascension and Jonathan, their guns at the ready, sought to pierce the murky gloom that surrounded us with their flashlights, but the darkness was somehow too powerful, almost as if it was alive, and yielded not an inch.

It didn't matter to me, because I knew how to find the entrance to Marie's estate. It was a white mansion surrounded by a terrace overlooking a small park just above the canals. Its slightly surelevated position had turned it into a small island, surrounded on all sides by the bayou's murky waters, the center of a veritable Sargasso of abandoned houses that were already plagued by death and rot.

I no longer benefited from the extra-sensory perceptions that the Key of Sakbata had briefly conferred upon me, but my instincts had never before misled me. I could tell that there was a miasmic evil lurking around Marie's estate, like a hostile army preparing to lay siege to a citadel.

Armed with the Key and the Dagger, Legendre had enough power to shake the world. I knew that he would not relent until he wrested the Cup of Erzulie from Marie as well. And I, playing ferryman to my friends like Charon on the River Styx, had the audacity of thinking I could beat him, assisted only by an old servant who had known better days, an untested young *vodunsi* and a lawyer who wanted to work for a *Fortune 500* corporation!

The folly of my undertaking was all too obvious to me; my chance of success was ridiculously low; but I didn't really have any other choice. My uncle thought I would become the legitimate heir of the Van Helsing line and follow in its traditions. He believed I would some day inherit—among other things—the talisman which he had been guarding. But I had let him down, just when he was counting on me the most. I hadn't been there for him. It occurred to me that I might now pay for that error of my wayward youth with my life, but I was a Van Helsing and this, I finally had realized, was my destiny. It had taken me a long time to learn that lesson, and I had made many, many mistakes in the process, but learn it I had—although it came too late to relieve my uncle of his burden. But it was not too late to repair some of those mistakes.

We were approaching Marie's property. I had no time left for self-pity. I wasn't surprised to discover that the massive iron gates that normally barred its entrance had been torn away like so much *papier-mâché*. It was as if a giant's hand had taken them and then crumpled them up. Only spikes of black iron emerged from the water to bar the entrance, like reefs around an atoll.

"We're here," I said.

Ascension was about to step off the boat and into the water when I stopped her with a gesture.

"Don't do that," I said.

I shook the pole I had been using to propel the boat around in the water and, suddenly, the pale light of the flashlights revealed the gaping jaws of an alligator which had been silently stalking us. The beast could have snapped the pole like a matchstick if I had tried using it against it.

"I don't know if it's a consequence of the hurricane, or if it's an effect of Legendre's magic, but I believe it would be unwise to step into the water at this time," I explained.

Ascension peered into the waters as if she were reading tea leaves.

"Normally, the snakes and the reptiles wouldn't attack a *houngan*," she said. "I think you're right; Legendre is behind this."

"But as far as we know, he doesn't have the Medallion of Damballah that would enable him to control reptiles..."

"What do we do?" asked Jonathan. "We can't stay here forever."

The problem was a simple one: we could enter the property only on foot, but that was prohibitively dangerous because of the creatures in the water.

"Let me help, M'sieur Hugo," said Zaka suddenly.

"What do you have in mind?" I asked.

"I know serpents; I used to breed them when I lived in Haiti. I even had a 'gator farm that tourists came from all over to see."

"Yes, but these 'gators aren't domesticated."

"There's no such thing as domesticated 'gators," he said, laughing. "It's something we say to make the tourists less afraid. With 'gators, you've got to be bigger than they are, that's all there's to it."

"Bigger than an alligator?" said Jonathan. "Is he crazy? Have you seen the size of that thing?"

"When the spirit of Danh-gbwe enters inside you, you become bigger than all the 'gators in the world," said Zaka.

Then, without a moment's hesitation, he jumped into the water and began to make an infernal racket.

"Danh-gbwe?" asked Jonathan.

"The great and powerful snake *loa* who acts as an intermediary for the Gods of Voodoo," replied Ascension.

In the water, Zaka was still thrashing around while singing some kind of hoarse incantation at the top of his lungs. I thought I recognized a recipe from Dahomey, but I must have been mistaken, because nothing more emerged from the water—snakes or alligators—to grab the old man and make him their dinner.

"Come on in!" Zaka eventually said, gesturing to us. "They're gone!"

It seemed incredible, but he'd done it!

We stepped into the dark, fetid waters which, at that spot, reached mid-thigh level. Fighting off nausea and the almost overwhelming compulsion to puke, we managed to carefully circle around the metal spikes and enter Marie Laveau's property.

We found ourselves in a forested garden full of majestic cypresses, overrun with Spanish moss, and red maples whose remaining foliage quivered in the wind, forming a canopy that conjured up the image of being inside a strange cathedral made of trees. As we advanced towards the highest point of the estate, the water level slowly dropped until it only reached our ankles. The sound of our boots slopping through mud and water-soaked vegetation was the only noise in the all-encompassing darkness. The silence was oppressive. There was no sign of life anywhere.

"We're here," I said, referring to a white mansion just beyond the curtain of the trees.

"And none too soon," complained Jonathan. "I thought we'd never leave that stinking jungle!"

"We're not alone," said Ascension suddenly.

I turned round and scanned the darkness that enveloped us. There was nobody and I heard nothing. The lights of our torches swept the park like the beams of a lighthouse in a storm, but they revealed nothing.

"Are you sure?" I asked.

She frowned and concentrated.

"I don't know," she finally admitted. "I hear a kind of rustling sound; it's almost imperceptible, like the contact of silk against skin..."

I didn't like it. I had an idea of what she might have been sensing, but I wasn't ready to share my suspicions with the others, at least not at that moment. I didn't want then to panic.

"Hurry up!" I said instead.

We rushed into a clearing and, at last, left the forest behind us. We ran across a vast lawn that ended on a magnificent terrace of white marble. It was located at the rear of Marie's house. Somehow, without realizing it, we had circled around the house during our journey through the gardens. That was odd in itself. Something, or someone, had interfered with my sense of direction. I guessed that, once again, Legendre was behind it...

We stepped onto the terrace and continued heading towards the house, leaving a series of muddy footprints behind us.

We arrived at a double glass door only to find it locked, of course. I rattled the handle without success.

"Let's not waste time," said Jonathan.

He used his AR-10 to try to smash the glass of the window, just like an action hero in some big screen blockbuster.

But in real life, it didn't work; the glass refused to break!

Jonathan hit it harder, this time using the butt of the weapon instead of the barrel.

Still nothing, not even the slightest crack!

The young lawyer looked at me in confusion.

"That's not possible! What kind of safety glass...?"

Meanwhile, Ascension was slowly and intently moving her long fingers across the window, looking like a blind person reading Braille.

"It's not safety glass," she said at last. "It's a protective spell that Marie has cast over her *hounfor*..."

She tapped the glass with her fingers, lightly playing a mysterious melody on an invisible keyboard.

"...But now that she knows we're here," she continued, "she'll let us in."

And as she said it, the door handle turned by itself, without any human intervention whatsoever!

I pushed the door and we entered the last refuge of the Voodoo Queen of New Orleans.

Without hesitation, I walked towards the stairs that led to Marie's sanctum, which I knew was on the first floor. It was the room where she performed all her rituals, with a beautiful view over the rest of the estate. Followed by my three companions, I climbed the steps of a marble staircase four at a time, then ran down a corridor decorated in the best Louis XV style, and which would not have been out of place in a Parisian *Hôtel Particulier* in the *Marais*.

Finally, I pushed against a double door and felt just like I had when, at nine, I had first experienced the extraordinary feeling of entering another world, another time.

Marie's *hounfor* was—or so I supposed—the faithful reconstruction of a temple from the legendary African city of Ife, which had disappeared more than 2000 years ago. Its adobe-like walls were decorated with paintings representing the Voodoo pantheon. The room was circular and, at its center, the great *mambo* stood before her altar. Only the vision of the nocturnal landscape of the forest that we could see through the large bay windows, where one would have logically expected to see the image of the African savanna, contrasted with the decor.

The atmosphere was permeated by a delicate smoke that smelled of forgotten spices and which came from a small fire burning on a three-legged brazier made of a dark red metal, which could well be orichalc. Marie Laveau stood at the center of the room, next to the altar, holding the Cup of Erzulie just as a priest holds a chalice during the Holy Mass. She was singing a melody in which I thought I recognized a few fragments of the Ancient Dogon tongue, which I had first decyphered from the scrolls of the *houngan* Temu, which are kept in the Invisible Archives of the Musée de l'Homme in Paris. I doubt that there were more than half a dozen anthropologists in the world capable of identifying this language, and none of us had ever heard it spoken. If I ever managed to make it out of there alive, I now could write a monograph on the use of the diphthong in the Dogon conditional tense that would surely earn me a flattering reputation in some academic quarters.

When she saw us enter, Marie stopped.

"Hugo! Ascension!" she said.

Her expression was a mixture of fatigue and relief.

"Oya!" Ascension exclaimed, rushing towards her mistress.

She reached her just in time, because the *mambo* began to shake and would have fallen if the young woman had not been there to support her.

"I did not want to involve you in this matter, my child," Marie said.

"I am your *vodunsi*, teacher," replied Ascension, looking slightly vexed. "It is my sacred duty to be at your side."

"Hugo Van Helsing," Marie said, now looking at me. "I was right on that day, when the *loa* revealed your destiny to me... You are the flame that pushes back the night, and the wind that drives away the pestilence, but the flame can become a fire and the wind a storm... As your ancestors did, you carry within you the seeds of destruction..."

She wasn't wrong. My family has, in fact, quite a few skeletons in its closets.

"I don't think the time is well-chosen to discuss our respective sins," I said. "Where is Legendre?"

She smiled, weakly, but the indomitable spirit that had earned her the title of Voodoo Queen continued to shine through her eyes.

"You are right," she said, sighing. "I have kept him in check since dawn, but he is powerful... More powerful than I..."

Knowing her pride, this admission only reinforced my fears.

"You gave him the Key of Sakbata," she looked at me in accusation.

"I didn't have any choice," I told her. "Besides, I had set a trap, but luck wasn't with me this time."

"Luck! You rely too much on luck, Hugo Van Helsing. The *loa* are fickle and, most often tend to favor the one who is the strongest. And in this fight, Legendre is the strongest."

"That's what he wants, of course, the Cup of Erzulie..." With a gesture, I pointed at the silver goblet that was still in her hand, before continuing: "...But why exactly? Possession of one or the other of those artifacts is enough to render its owner virtually immortal. What more can he want? Does he want to use the power of Voodoo to rule Haiti, as Mayes and Duvalier did? The

Key of Sakbata alone would be enough for that, as it was in the past. I don't understand what..."

"Legendre seeks the *baru áva togu nà*."

"The *báru*...? But that's a purely ceremonial ritual, without any effect other than the symbolic, a confirmation by the Gods of a purely mental state, nothing more."

"Don't tell me that you, a *vodunsi* who studied with the great Soulagé Minfort, subscribe to the theories of the symbolist school. I'm shocked."

"As I said before, I don't think this is the appropriate time to discuss our respective sins," I said. "The interpretations of the symbolist school seem to me more valid when analyzing the majority of the relevant Voodoo phenomena. But, in this case, I'm ready to revise my opinion and accept a traditionalist version."

"What are you two talking about?" asked Jonathan, interrupting us. "What does all that *mumbo jumbo* have to do with Legendre?"

I smiled, because I found it ironic that our young attorney was annoyed over a technical discussion taking place between two professionals. Meanwhile, Ascension, too, sought to understand the meaning of Marie's words.

"*Togu nà?*" she asked. "The great people?"

"No, child," said Mary, correcting her emphasis on *togu*. "The House of the Word. The Place of Judgment."

"What judgment?" Jonathan asked, increasingly frustrated.

"*Báru áva*. The Judgment of Masks," said Ascension. "New Orleans. I begin to understand..."

"Legendre... Very bad man," opined Zaka, shaking his head.

I hastened to explain the meaning of all of it to our young lawyer before he had another fit of pique.

"It's an old Voodoo ritual, which dates back to ancient times. Something that many experts regard as purely symbolic, like the Sacrament of the Eucharist, for example... In reality, you do not eat the flesh of Christ, nor do you drink His blood during Communion; it's purely symbolic. That's why the Church invented the notion of transubstantiation. In this instance, according to Marie, it would seem that the symbolists were wrong and that the ritual does correspond, in fact, to something quite tangible..."

Marie nodded vehemently. She had just won a major victory in a dispute between experts from two opposing schools; I noted in passing that she wasn't showing a great deal of magnanimity in her triumph. I continued:

"...*Báru* is the Judgment of the Gods, and *áva* the Gathering of Masks, in this case, a symbolic representation of the human race. It is interesting to note that, because of its Carnival, New Orleans is traditionally regarded as a city of masks and therefore particularly suitable to being chosen as the *togu nà*, the House of the Word, where Man can petition the Gods directly and ask them to render their judgment..."

"Legendre... Very bad man," Zaka said.

"I still don't see where all this is going," said Jonathan.

But his worried expression made me realize that he had begun to accept that there was more behind what was going on than the twisted fantasies of a delusional Haitian witch doctor.

"I'm getting there," I said. "Legendre wants to summon the Voodoo Gods, which is why he needs their Talismans, and ask them to make him their equal."

"What do you mean, equal?"

"Godlike. Not just symbolically either," I said, nodding to Marie, to acknowledge that she had been right all along, "but literally. Legendre will become a God—if the other Gods permit it, of course."

The young lawyer now looked rather haggard. All this was obviously taking a toll.

"Permit it?"

"The *báru áva* requires sacrifices," said Marie. "Great sacrifices. The hurricane itself is the sacrifice offered by Legendre to Hevioso, the God of Thunder. That will please him. I have no doubt that Ascension is the sacrifice he plans to offer Erzulie, if he seizes the Cup... That's why I tried to keep you out of all this, child," added to the *mambo* to the young girl.

"I understand, Oya, but Legendre has not yet won, and my blood is not yet ready to be offered to Erzulie."

"What about the sacrifice offered to Sakbata?" asked Jonathan.

"Here it comes," I said, designating the bay window.

And, in the light of the Moon, we saw the ugly horde of the zombies, freshly dug up corpses, some partially eaten by alligators, others murdered by looters, who hadn't even had time to know the peace of the grave. Their pale and sinister faces, their empty orbits and flabby flesh pierced by bones whose whiteness stood out against the ambient darkness, moved slowly to the rhythm of a music that only they could hear.

The dead of Katrina had become a macabre army reanimated by the Key of Sakbata, the God of Death and Pestilence set in motion at the behest of Legendre, the cursed *houngan*, and were marching towards the house of Marie Laveau.

THIS LAND WAS BUILT WITH THE BLOOD OF OUR PEOPLE.

Once the Cup of Erzulie was in his possession, and filled with the blood of Marie—or Ascension—Legendre could force the Goddess to obey the invocations of the person who held her Talisman, and make her uphold Hevioso and Sakbata's judgments in his favor.

The three Voodoo Gods would then make him a God.

The prospect was not particularly pleasing; indeed, it was frankly appalling. It was enough to remember the atrocities committed by Papa Doc Duvalier, a mortal man, with the power of a single Talisman, to imagine the nightmarish crimes that Legendre could commit with the power of a God at his disposal.

Outside, the terrace had been overrun by the zombies, who were scratching at the doors and windows like rats trying to infiltrate a pantry.

The analogy was not entirely inappropriate, and what it suggested was enough to make one's blood run cold as ice.

The skepticism of our friend Jonathan seemed to have left him, because he was casting panicked glances in all directions. His tongue distractedly wet his lips. He had the unmistakable look of a trapped animal desperately seeking a way out. I couldn't say that I blamed him.

Ascension and I, being more experienced in this field, knew that the supernatural protections erected by the *mambo*, would not be so easily broken by mere zombies. They were, after all, only Legendre's puppets. The Haitian *houngan* was our real problem.

I searched the darkness and, suddenly, I saw him. Legendre. He was dressed as he had been at the Cemetery the day before; he looked like a scarecrow and the tattered black frockcoat floating behind him in the wind gave his gangly silhouette a particularly sinister look.

In his hands, he held the Dagger of Hevioso and the Key of Sakbata. He radiated the power of darkness.

The hordes of zombies parted to let him pass.

There he stood, in the center of the terrace, totally silent for several seconds before bursting loudly into a wild and raucous laugh.

"Marie Laveau!" he screamed. "I know you're in there, witch! I smell the rancid odor of your ancient skin."

He sniffed the air, just like a hungry beast, before continuing:

"You are not alone. The Van Helsing and his friends are with you. I can smell their fear, the fear of the white man before his master. Tell them that they will know peace soon enough. In a few minutes, my zombies will have feasted upon their flesh and they, too, will join my army of the living dead."

An alluring program, if I ever I'd heard one!

Marie was not intimidated by Legendre. She had seen her share of madmen during her millennia-long life. She opened the bay window and stepped out onto a small balcony outside. The zombies reacted to her presence by drooling on, clawing and ripping at each other like a pack of jackals confronted by its prey.

"You are nothing more than a mongrel dog, Legendre," she said. "You will die like your ancestor, cursed, and your soul will join his in the infernal marshes. You will spend eternity counting the eggs of the flies hatching on your naked eyes..."

She had style. If she had sought to provoke Legendre, she was successful. The *houngan* spat and uttered an abominable blaspheme, which, if I am to believe the *Malleus Maleficarum*, had gotten a Dominican monk burned at the stake in 1476. Then he shouted:

"You call yourself the Voodoo Queen! Your servants call you Oya, as it was on the land of our ancestors, but you..."

Marie interrupted him:

"*Our* ancestors, Legendre? Your mother was only a poor child, driven half-crazy after being raped by the white sorcerer whose name you bear and who stole our secrets. In Ancient Ife, you would not even have been deemed worthy to defile one of our temples! Your life itself is an insult to the *loa*! Poor fool who believes that the Gods will make him one of their own! Wake up, Legendre! Yield now while there is still time..."

Suddenly, she changed her tone, trying to appeal to his reason and his vanity:

"...You already hold two of our most sacred Talismans. The years that you have to live now are as numerous as the grains of sand in the sea. Your power is immense, I admit it, but you do not take into account the extent of the evil forces that you have unleashed. Think. Reconsider. It is not too late."

For a brief moment, I wondered if her arguments had hit a chord, because when Legendre spoke again, he did not seem nearly as self-confident as he had before.

"I will be a God, Marie Laveau," he said. "It is my destiny."

Marie shook her head.

"The Gods have gone," she replied.

"Because their priests were weak, like you. They lost their faith, forgot their true duties and thought only of their privileges. But the Gods will return when I call them and, together, we will reshape this Lower World and what was past will live again."

"He is crazy," whispered Marie. Then, in a loud voice, she said: "The Gods left because the World turned."

Legendre sniggered:

"Which World? This one? This land was built with the blood of our people who were torn from our ancient homeland. It's our own blood and the dust of our bones that hold up their accursed cities. This World is already dead, Oya! Its own white masters have sacrificed it on the altar of their mercantile appetites. The time of the Judgment of Masks has come. This very Moon, I will kill millions of white men and women to offer Sakbata a worthy sacrifice—a blood sacrifice worthy of Hevioso, Damballah and Erzulie and they will consecrate me their equal!"

Suddenly, without my being able to either anticipate his gesture, or stop him, Jonathan drew his gun. In a re-markably swift and precise gesture, he shot twice and two bullets smashed into Legendre's head.

The back of the evil *houngan*'s skull exploded, but he only laughed. I had seen many horrible events in my life, but the vision of that macabre figure, half of his head blown away, cackling in the night was one of the most sinister.

Legendre brandished the Key of Sakbata and shouted:

"Fools! This Key makes me the master of Life and Death!"

He had a point: how could you actually kill someone who is beyond life and death?

Jonathan shrugged.

"It was worth a try," he said.

"I was about to try something like that myself," agreed Marie.

"Do I conclude that our attempts at negotiations have failed?" I asked.

In response, Legendre, brandishing his two Talismans, unleashed a spell, the effect of which was overwhelming and immediate. Marie looked as if she had been struck by lightning. Her hands were clutching the Cup of Erzulie so hard that they became white. She, too, began to sing a spell, then she whispered:

"A... Ascension..."

The young woman rushed to her side at once. She also grasped the Cup with her delicate hands and began to sing the same song her mistress was singing. The two voices combined to strengthen the spell, but it was already too late.

There was a silent explosion in the air—not an explosion that could be perceived with any of the normal five senses, but one that was heard only within the depths of one's soul. I would have sworn that I glimpsed a color that I will never be able to describe, smelled garlic, heard a distant horn and the beating of the wings of a dove...

The supernatural protection which Mary had erected around her house immediately collapsed.

"Go, my children!" Legendre screamed. "New flesh awaits you within these walls! Feast upon it!"

The zombies launched an uncoordinated assault on the house, breaking through all its doors and windows. Nothing inside could escape their insatiable appetite.

"Do you have a plan?" Jonathan asked me.

"Not really," I answered. "My plan was, and still is, to stop Legendre, but that's not as simple as I initially thought. That said, I haven't lost all hope..."

"Zombies!" he screamed. "A hundred zombies are coming after us to eat us! You heard Legendre? And that's the best you can do?"

"Well, it's true that they are zombies, yes," I said. "But contrary to popular belief, zombies aren't usually cannibals, nor particularly dangerous. What they really want is to return to the peace of their graves, which they were forced to leave. Generally, they're really pretty docile, the ideal slave labor, but completely lacking in initiative. In ordinary circumstances we could simply ignore them and they wouldn't touch us. But, in this case, what makes our situation rather precarious is that they are being driven by Legendre's desires, at least as long as he controls the power of Sakbata..."

"So then what are we going to do? Do you have a plan to stop them?"

I gently tapped the butt of my AR-10.

"This is my plan," I said. "Aim for the head."

"The head?"

"It won't kill them—it's impossible to kill a zombie—but it should slow them down and keep us safe. Otherwise, use the machetes."

While Zaka and Jonathan set up a summary barricade in front of the door of the sanctuary that now served as our refuge, I turned towards Marie.

"It makes no sense to stay cooped up in here," I said. "Time is against us. The only enemy that really counts is Legendre. We have to go outside and confront him on his own ground, otherwise we're lost—not to mention the rest of New Orleans, and, who knows, maybe the whole country as well."

"What do you suggest?" asked the *mambo*.

"First, Ascension and you need to create some kind of diversion. We'll never reach Legendre if his zombies bar the way."

"And then what?"

"Then? I'm convinced that Legendre made a fundamental mistake..."

"What mistake?" asked Ascension.

"Marie was right just now: the Voodoo Gods left because the nature of things has changed. It might be possible that all the magic of Voodoo and a human sacrifice immense enough could, for a brief moment on a cosmic scale, turn the tide of history and force the return of the Gods, but I doubt it. There are powers in the Universe that are above even those of the Gods, and which they fear themselves. An... *arbitration* by Mawu-Lisa, the Supreme Godhead of the Voodoo, might work."

Marie looked at me thoughtfully. I smiled at her a little sheepishly and continued:

"The advantage of the symbolist school is that we become accustomed to thinking in abstract terms and give free rein to our imaginations. I bet Legendre is a traditionalist."

The *mambo* gave me a venomous look.

"I don't understand," said Ascension.

"Let's say that I have faith in Destiny, whether it is called Mawu-Lisa, Ananke, Dahaka or Niobe. We can't let Legendre be the only one to invoke the Gods; we have to be able to plead our cause, as well. So, now we need a diversion to get out of here, because at the moment, all my beautiful plans remain virtual if we don't get down there soon..."

But it was already too late. The blows and the scratching on the other side of the double door told us that the zombies had found us. The sound of their nails dragging and tearing against the teak was as bearable as the screech of chalk on a blackboard.

A blow, more violent than the others, popped one half of the door off its hinges.

Jonathan whacked the first zombie in the head with a well-timed shot. He had to have been first in his class at the shooting range.

Other zombies followed into the breach. I saw Zaka chop off a flaccid arm with a *coupe-chou* which he had found hanging on the wall.

Despite his energetic blows, and Jonathan's aggressive defense, it was clearly only a matter of minutes before the zombies would all get through. They had the numbers in their favor.

Already a few had managed to climb over the barricade. It was my turn to fire. I was sick of seeing the virtually headless bodies continue to crawl towards us, their nails scraping against the floor like so many horrible, hairy-legged spiders.

"You have to do something!" I said, turning towards Marie. "Otherwise, we've had it."

The Voodoo Queen approved with a nod of her head. Then she grabbed Ascension and told her:

"The time of the *yanakundu* has come, child."

Ascension opened her eyes wide.

"The *yanakundu*, Mistress?" she whispered. "The ritual transfer... You cannot... You should not. I am not worthy..."

Marie took the young woman's hand, almost forcibly, and placed it firmly on the Cup of Erzulie. Then she began a new ritual, in a hoarse voice that was gut-wrenching to hear.

I was not a neophyte and I well knew the sacrifice that she was making. The Voodoo Gods are no more philanthropic than any of the other Gods. Every action requires a reaction. Marie put her life in the balance by choosing her successor, then transferring her powers. If things went wrong, Ascension would soon find herself the new Earthly Incarnation of the Goddess Erzulie...

Immediately, the air in the room seemed to become heavier, as if it had gained some kind of thicker consistency. Indeed, the movements of the zombies became even slower. When I extended my arm to take advantage of this and shoot one of the living dead, I, too, felt that I was moving in slow motion, as if I was at the bottom of a swimming pool. Even my bullet seemed to emerge from the gun barrel more slowly than the laws of physics would allow.

Within this *liquid air* in which we moved, I saw silhouettes thrashing and twisting. They were semi-transparent, with a degree of refraction slightly more than that of water; allowing me to see them vaguely and ascertain their contours when they passed in front of a person or thing.

I guessed that Marie's spell had—temporarily, I hoped—removed one of the barriers that separate our reality from the more "etheric" plane which was the realm of the spirits that surround us. The things that I saw moving amongst us in this bizarre slow-time were the *loa* themselves!

Marie appeared to be negotiating with them and, judging from her face, it did not seem to be an easy task. Her features were drawn and beads of sweat were trickling down her cheeks. I remembered what she had said earlier: *The* loa *are fickle and, most often, tend to favor the one who is the strongest.* Was Marie Laveau still the unchallenged Voodoo Queen?

I saw her brandish the Cup of Erzulie, waving it amongst the *loa* like scepter, Ascension's hand never leaving hers, drawing from the young girl's strength, shouting the name of Erzulie. I didn't know what unimaginable threats she uttered, or what mysterious entreaties she proffered, but her arguments seemed to be bearing fruit, because, suddenly, I saw the *loa* harden, lose their transparency and fully materialize on our plane. The air lost its mysterious *liquid* consistency and returned to normal.

The *loa* had adopted various animal forms, mixing species to create chimeras, such as a lion-headed snake and a winged crocodile.

Our supernatural allies threw themselves on the zombies. I would not say they became easy prey—that would be an exaggeration—but they bought us enough time to leave the *hounfor* before it became a death trap.

Accompanied—preceded even—by our *guardian angels*, we ran down the corridor. Jonathan wanted to use the grand staircase that we had taken to get to the first floor, but I stopped him:

"If we want to catch Legendre by surprise, it's better to take an alternative route. Follow me! I know this place like the back of my hand."

I had spent plenty time playing hide and seek here as a kid and that gave me the knowledge I needed. I then noticed that Marie was out of breath. Her complexion had become frighteningly ashy. This was extraordinarily unusual and, for the first time, I experienced the very real fear that we might not emerge victorious from our confrontation with the Haitian *houngan*. As I feared, the *loa* had requested—and received—a very high price for their help...

"This way," I said, taking the lead of our little group.

We continued our flight through a series of corridors and a large library, quite comparable to that of my uncle, before locating a small, well-hidden staircase which I knew led to the kitchen.

The zombies continued to shamble after us, making a hellish racket. Behind me, I heard the macabre swishing sound of Zaka's machete and Jonathan's short bursts of gunfire. The floor became sticky with blood and stank from the mixture of different organs and fluids that come from the decomposition of the human body. One thing that is never mentioned in the zombie movies that I'd seen was their stench.

We made use of the valuable furniture collected by Marie over the centuries to slow our adversaries, but such flimsy obstacles barely slowed them down. A zombie suddenly sprang up in front of me, coming out of a room which I hadn't noticed. Fortunately, he stumbled on the shattered remains of a beautiful First Empire secretary. That gave me time to reload my gun and blow out his brains. When he fell, he broke a magnificent vase from the Tang Dynasty and I couldn't help but feel a pinch of the my heart.

We finally made it to the kitchen.

In front of me, as if it had been vomited by the very mouth of Hell, stood yet one more zombie, who had had to be a true giant of a man when he was alive. His body, a muscle-bound hulk, was covered by a strange and slimy melange of bile and pus. His jaws made spasmodic movements like those of a beast in the process of rooting through the earth. I imagined that he had been buried anonymously in a bayou or some swamp, perhaps as the result of a criminal execution, and had spent some time digging himself out. His eyes glowed but otherwise showed no human expression.

The zombie moved towards Ascension, who was paralyzed with terror. His clawed arms tried to grasp the young woman's hair, perhaps in response to an ancient memory. His mouth, with its rows of rotten teeth, made a foul, masticating sound; its slobbering froth left a disgusting trail of equally foul-smelling slime behind.

Instinctively, without even being aware that I did it, I threw Ascension out of his way. Better to have a few bruises on her knees and elbows than the monstrous fate that would have otherwise been hers! Then, I fired my gun, twice, and despite the relative obscurity of the kitchen, managed to place two bullets square in the creature's head. It exploded—or rather, half of it exploded, only half! Its body was shaken by a long and powerful tremor. What remained of its mouth contracted and expanded under the convulsions. His arms still clawed at the empty air with a vengeful greed. The creature now moved towards me with indomitable fury, even causing the ground beneath its feet to shake. Zaka arrived at my rescue with his machete; he grabbed the head of the monster by its long, stinking hair, then swung his blade and decapitated it.

The zombie's head crashed and broke like a rotten pumpkin, revealing a tumefied brain, already half liquefied. But the magic of Sakbata remained powerful. Even without its head, the monster still barred our way and was still capable killing us!

I took one of the grenades we'd taken from Uncle Ohisver's private arsenal from my belt; it was similar to the one which I had tried to use to send Legendre to join his questionable ancestors. With a quick gesture, and careful to avoid the zombie's hands, I rammed it inside the thing's neck cavity, then I made a sign that the others should back off quickly. Almost immediately, an explosion destroyed the zombie's trunk, and its remains fell heavily to the ground. The creature jerked a few times, then finally stopped. A viscous, black liquid oozed from its carcass.

We crossed the kitchen without further incident and arrived in a large dining room which had bay windows that overlooked the gardens.

It was midnight. The sky was a pure, velvety black; we could see the stars perfectly. It was always like that after a hurricane. We were almost at the New Moon, and without the light pollution normally created by the city, the scene was illuminated by a strange, heavenly light.

Legendre still stood in the center of the terrace, the true embodiment of death. He was now surrounded by miasma of energy in which I could vaguely see two humanoid forms: Hevioso and Sakbata, in the process of materializing in preparation for the Judgment of Masks. We didn't have much time.

"It is time to be heard," said Marie, brandishing the Cup of Erzulie.

"You know the risks?" I asked.

"I do."

"Sakbata and Hevioso now stand alongside Legendre. Even if you have the support of Erzulie... To have any chance of prevailing, we would need the Medallion of Damballah..."

"I know," she said, resignedly. "But have it, we do not. I have no choice." Then she turned to Ascension and said: "Come, child."

"Yes, Oya, but...?"

"You are now the Incarnation of Erzulie, just as I am. The ritual of *yanakundu* consecrated you to the Goddess. You must stand proudly by my side when we challenge the will of the Gods."

Ascension looked at me. I remembered that she was my cousin. The pain in my heart was all the greater when I realized that she was very likely walking to her death.

"Hugo," she asked. "What will happen if...?"

I didn't have the heart to tell her. If the Gods rejected Marie's petition, even Erzulie would have to concede, and I very much doubted that her Incarnations would survive such a resolution.

It was now up to Jonathan, Zaka and I to ensure the safety of Marie and Ascension during the Judgment of Masks.

Suddenly, I realized that Jonathan was no longer with us!

In our wild ride through Marie's house, we had somehow lost our young lawyer. Had he fallen victim to the zombies? If so, there was nothing more I could do for him. I shouted his name several times, unfortunately without success.

Like Zigor, he had become another casualty of our battle. I felt a mixture of rage and impotence.

Well, Zaka and I would have to mount our little Alamo on our own, without Jonathan. However, I wasn't taking bets on our chances of getting out alive.

Meanwhile, Marie and Ascension, holding hands, had walked out onto the terrace. Marie held the Cup of Erzulie before her.

As the two women approached Legendre, the Cup began to radiate the same energy as the Key and the Dagger. The vortex surrounding Legendre grew bigger, pulsating and expanding to include the two women. I then distinguished a third form, vaguely humanoid, which materialized alongside the two others. It was difficult, if not downright impossible, for a man to truly grasp the nature of the Gods. Our five senses are entirely insufficient. Barely at the limits of my Earthly perception, I first saw something that looked like a bee, or a flower, or perhaps nothing I could really recognize... I heard a noise, like that of a radio vainly trying to tune into a far-away station in the middle of a thunderstorm... Ethereal voices spoke directly into my mind...

"Erzulie. Mother of Poisons. Sister of Flowers. You have finally joined us..."

"Sakbata, my Dark Baron... Hevioso, Lord of Thunder... We are all together again..."

A thunderous voice replied:

"Not all. Our Brother the Serpent is not yet amongst us."

And the voice of Erzulie answered:

"Not yet."

I didn't have time to reflect on the enigmatic meaning of her words because Zaka called me:

"M'sieur Hugo!"

It was a good thing he had gotten my attention, because the zombies had recovered and were all too willing to turn us into a midnight snack.

Without further ado, I fired, hitting one of the creatures in the neck. Its head separated from its body and rolled on the ground. I pulled back to escape the claws of another creature, which Zaka then decapitated with his machete.

But the undead surrounded us on all sides. Our shots only slowed down their advance. Sooner or later, they would overtake us, but I thought that our deaths would be worth it if Marie and Ascension could stop Legendre...

"This isn't going well," I said to Zaka, adjusting my shooting so as not to unnecessarily waste ammunition.

My target, another zombie, collapsed on the ground, joining his fellows in a noisy pile where limbs tore at each other in a stinking charnel.

"Do you still have some grenades left?" Zaka asked.

"Only one; it won't be enough to get rid of them all," I replied.

The old man slaughtered another zombie.

"If the shockwave mows down a large enough number, perhaps we can escape? Our job here is finished anyway..."

I grabbed my last grenade and I was about to throw it into the zombies' midst when suddenly, I heard:

"Hu... go..."

It was Zigor Side!

Zigor, resurrected! Zigor, who had risen from the makeshift morgue of our cold room suddenly stood before me!

Tuesday, August 30

GODS ARE LIKE LAWYERS.

I felt as if I was paralyzed. I raised my arm to strike Zigor, to smash his grinning, zombie head, but I couldn't. I just couldn't!

Zaka and I were now completely surrounded by the zombies.

On the terrace, I still could see Marie and Ascension facing Legendre in the Council of the Gods, insulated from our mundane reality by strange, unfathomable energies. Even though I had no clue as to whether or not they were being successful in arguing our case, I didn't feel optimistic. Could they still win the day?

I raised my arm again to strike Zigor down. He was a zombie. He couldn't talk; I was sure I'd just had an auditory hallucination because of all the stress. There was no time to lose; I had to destroy him before he destroyed me.

But then, the impossible occurred again: I saw his lips move.

"Hu... go," he groaned.

Somewhere deep within his vitreous eyes—there was no doubt those eyes belonged to a dead man—I began to think that I saw a spark of recognition, of awareness, but I kept telling myself that it wasn't possible! It went against everything we knew about zombies. Yet, wasn't it conceivable that even Sakbata's fearsome magic couldn't succeed in entirely eradicating the deep, lasting friendship that had bound Zigor and me?

I rebelled against my own mind, it was a preposterous notion! Zombies had no feelings, no emotions, no thought or desire for anything except carnage. Zigor's half-slit throat, still oozing blood and other unspeakable fluids, was right in front of me, it's very existence confirming his true nature. No other proof was needed.

I raised my arm again to strike him down.

Another zombie shambled forward, his slobbering jaws already open and chewing, clearly announcing his intentions. Suddenly, with superhuman strength, Zigor's fist smashed into the creature's face, causing his head to explode.

I just didn't know what to believe anymore.

"Hu...go... stop... behaving... like a jerk," said Zigor, enouncing his words with difficulty.

That huge gash in his neck couldn't have made it easy for him to speak, I thought.

My dead lawyer then turned around and, facing the other zombies, issued a supernatural shout, the type of bellowing howl that could only be produced by a God—and, as later events proved, I wasn't wrong in drawing that conclusion, but I'm getting ahead of myself.

Whether or not it was a God that had spoken through Zigor, the other zombies got the message and pulled back. They began to wander about aimlessly, chewing on bits of flesh and bones without any real passion or purpose.

I kept staring at my friend Zigor—my friend the zombie—and finally asked:

"Zigor... By what miracle...?"

"You didn't think I was going to let you stew in this mess all by yourself? Hell, no! What are friends for? You can't get rid of me that easily. I'm on a retainer."

"But... you're a—a zombie?"

"No shit, Sherlock. You don't miss a thing, do you? But you're right. It is kind of weird that I'm back. Freaky weird, even for me, if I do say so myself."

"Why are you back?"

"Yeah, freaky all right... I'm here to deliver a message..."

"From whom?" I asked.

"From Sammy," he replied.

"Sammy?"

"Yeah... You know him as Baron Samedi, but he's really a simple guy at heart, not a pompous bastard like those guys from the Disciplinary Review Board... Not pretentious at all."

"Sakbata," I said. "You spoke to Sakbata, the God of Death. How?"

"It's kind of complicated to explain, especially to someone who isn't dead. If you were dead, it'd be way easier. Hey, I don't mean to say I wish you were dead or anything. No, no, no, not at all. That's not what I meant at all. But it's hard to describe... When you're dead, Sammy, he's like that upstairs neighbor who parties all night with his stereo blaring all the time. When you knock on the ceiling, he's going to come down pronto. You get it?"

"Not really," I said. "What does he want?"

"Who?"

"Sakbata."

"Who's Sakbata?"

His new condition had definitely not improved his mental faculties; it was like talking to your brother-in-law when he was high.

"Sammy," I said.

"Shit, yeah, Sammy. What did he want? It's hard for me to remember things..."

"You mentioned a message?"

"Everything was so much clearer in the Savanna."

I had had quite a number of nonsensical conversations in my life, some while I was under the influence of peyote, but this was turning out by far to be the craziest.

"What savanna?"

"Where Sammy and the others go to rest..." There was a long pause, during which I presumed he gathered whatever was left of his wits, then he continued: "I've got to tell you, Hugo. Gods are like lawyers. They come if you call them when you're in trouble, they take care of the mess, they get paid and then, they leave, either because someone else needs them, or to go on vacation in the Bahamas. It's the same for Sammy and the others, José, Izzie..."

"Hevioso, Erzulie."

"Right, those guys. They have other humanities who need them more than we, now. Younger Earths where the human race is still in its cradle. And when they're not working, they're relaxing on the Savanna, in the Great Beyond. They know we don't need them anymore, but they're still connected to our world through ancient covenants. It's like when I gave my business card to that girl in El Paso, who was turning tricks on the side. It took me three years to get rid of her... Anyway, Legendre is starting to seriously get on their nerves. They'd like to get rid of him and head back to the Savanna."

In the end, it would seem that neither the symbolist nor the traditionalist schools were right. As always, reality was both simpler and far more complex than imagined.

"If that's the case," I asked, "why don't they just tell him to go and take a hike?"

"Didn't you listen to me? I told you: there are ancient covenants that are still in force. Being a lawyer, I understand that. Laws remain on the books for a long time, even when they fall into disuse. When an Incarnation uses one of the talismans to summon his God, he or she must come. They don't have a choice."

"I see. So they sent you back to help me stop Legendre?"

If a zombie could ever look embarrassed, I swore Zigor was it.

"Er, not quite," he said. "They know you, Hugo, they like you all right, but you're not the one they want—it's him they need."

Zigor pointed at the person who stood next to me.

"Zaka?" I said, not daring to understand the full extent of the picture that was beginning to form in my mind.

"Yeah. It turns out that the old guy is the incarnation of Damballah."

"Zaka—the incarnation of Damballah?"

Zigor smiled a crooked smile, since half of his face was still a death mask.

"If you keep repeating everything I say, someone's gonna think you're the zombie, Hugo. Yeah, Zaka. Sammy wants him to join them, because without his help, they won't be able to get rid of Legendre. There are four talismans. The four Gods have to be present again, like they were at the beginning."

138

What he said made plenty of sense. My instincts had not been wrong: we had to rely on the Gods' sense of destiny, but I would never have imagined that the solution to our problem had been so close to us from the very beginning.

I turned towards Zaka and asked:

"Is this true?"

I didn't really have any doubts, but I needed to hear it from him.

"Yes, M'sieur Hugo," he said, "but I won't join them. I don't want to be the incarnation of the Devil again. I renounced the religion of my ancestors long ago. I've converted to Catholicism. I'm a good Christian now. I've renounced the Devil and all his works..."

In a flash, I understood then that Zaka had been born in Africa, in the Land of the Ancestors, like Marie, a long, long time ago... Was he Wedo, the original owner of the Medallion of Damballah, or someone who had inherited it later? The answers would likely remain forever hidden. But one thing was certain: at one time, he had been evangelized by the Missionaries and had renounced the Old Religion, forsaken Damballah for Christianity. Without him, the God could not incarnate—and Legendre would triumph.

"Zaka," I said, "this isn't the time for sectarian disputes. You do understand that if you refuse to allow Damballah to appear, thousands of people are going to die?"

"Damballah is the Devil, M'sieur Hugo. Father Merrin explained it all to me. If I use the Medallion, I'm enabling the Devil to walk the Earth again. That would make me the Antichrist. I can't do it!"

I never thought ill of Missionaries as a rule, but this was one time when I really wished they had stayed home rather then convert one of the four Incarnations of Voo-doo. Why couldn't Father Merrin mind his own god-damn business...?

"Zaka... Listen to me..."

I tried desperately to find some argument that would convince him, but without success.

"Take it easy, Hugo," said Zigor. "Sammy thought of everything. I brought someone with me that will get him to change his mind."

Zigor snapped his finger, as if he was calling a waiter over in a restaurant. Considering the advanced state of decomposition his body was in, the sound it made was disgustingly squishy and, for a second, I feared that his little display of bravura might cost him his hand.

A zombie stepped away from the rest of the unliv-ing horde and, slowly and painfully, dragged himself towards us. He was dressed like a corpse fresh from the Morgue, in a knee-length blue gown. With the New Moon, the light was not sufficient for me to see his face, but despite that, something in his appearance—perhaps his walk? Or a vague family air?—made me immedi-ately guess who he was.

"Uncle Ohisver!"

"Hugo."

I almost couldn't believe my eyes. The power of Sakbata had pulled Uncle Ohisver from his slab and brought him here.

"Your friend owes me 40 bucks," said my uncle with the sly smile that I knew so well, pointing at Zigor.

"We played a hand or two of poker while waiting for Sammy," explained the lawyer.

Ohisver then turned towards Zaka:

"Zaka... My good master... I beseech you, I who faithfully served you all my days..."

And I then realized that I, like everyone else, had always assumed, when looking at my rich, white uncle, and his poor, black companion, that the latter was the former's servant, when in fact, it had been the opposite!

It wasn't Zaka who was my uncle's servitor, but Ohisver who had served Zaka!

From their conversation, I gathered that Uncle Ohisver had met Zaka in Haiti, around the time of the death of Buonaparte Ignace Gallia, the twisted *houngan* who had killed his father, Ruven Van Helsing. It was even possible that Zaka had played a part in Gallia's demise.

In any event, Uncle Ohisver had identified Zaka as the incarnation of Damballah and had decided to serve him, as a disciple serves a master of the craft. After Gallia's death, when my uncle inherited the Key of Sakbata, it was Zaka, ever the good Christian, who had convinced him to not use its power to become the incarnation of the dreaded Baron Samedi, but instead to hide it carefully and make sure no one else could use it for evil ends.

"Zaka," said my uncle, "I know that I'm asking you to sacrifice your life, to end your immortal existence..."

"My life doesn't matter, M'sieur Ohisver," said Zaka. "I already know that it has reached its end. The blessed Saints themselves have appeared to me in a dream to tell me that my time has come. I'm willing to sacrifice even my very soul, but..."

"But what?"

"I can't be the incarnation of the Devil (he meant Damballah) by myself. I'm too old. Like Marie, I have to have a *vodunsi*. And I didn't want to sacrifice *his* soul..."

He had no need to say whose soul he meant; his eyes looking at me, full of deep and sincere affection, were all the explanation I required.

"Hugo," said my uncle, also looking at me. "My nephew."

I had known that there was yet more to it than what he had told us; it wasn't his immortal soul that he was worried about, *it was mine!*

And yet, I couldn't let Legendre win.

"Zaka," I said, "I'm incredibly moved, more than I can say, but it has to be my decision, not yours. I'm more than ready to throw my soul in the balance to stop the horror and the carnage that Legendre will unleash. I am willing to be your *vodunsi*."

"But it will cost you your soul, M'sieur Hugo."

"I know, but wasn't even your Savior willing to sacrifice Himself to redeem the rest of humanity?"

"Yes, but..."

"You're right, Zaka," my uncle said suddenly. "Hugo won't be your *vodunsi*."

"Uncle Ohisver?"

"From... where I was... I saw many things, Hugo. I saw your work. I learned that you had become a worthy member of our family. In fact, you have within you the potential to become the greatest of all the Van Helsing line. But your role is not to become the incarnation of Damballah. Another one has been chosen for that function... That's why Sakbata sent him back to us."

Zigor?

If I had understood him correctly, my dead lawyer was to be Zaka's *vodunsi*?

"Hey, that's cool with me," said Zigor. "Incarnation of Damballah. Try to beat that on a résumé. I can't wait until the next alumni meeting at Harvard. In your face, Dershowitz!"

Zaka scrutinized Zigor, and when I said scrutinized, I mean that he looked deep within my lawyer's soul. In fact, Zigor must have had some previously unsuspected depths, because it took what felt like a very long time.

Finally, Zaka extracted a small gold medal from the clutter of the other religious amulets he wore on chains hanging on his chest.

The Medallion of Damballah!

I remembered the lessons of Edgar Allan Poe's *Purloined Letter*. If you want to hide something where no one will ever think of looking for it, do it in plain sight, preferably among other similar, ordinary-looking objects.

Zaka then asked Zigor if he was ready. My lawyer nodded. Considering the slash across his neck, he couldn't have been much more demonstrative without running the risk of losing his head for good. But his feelings came across without ambiguity.

Zaka took Zigor's hand in his, and holding the Medallion in the other, went through the same ritual of *yanakundu* that had earlier bound Ascension and Marie together.

The Medallion began to radiate the same otherworldly light as the Cup of Erzulie.

Zaka and Zigor then walked towards the Council of the Gods. As they reached it, the energy vortex swelled up to swallow them and admit them inside. I was barely able to distinguish a fourth shape—that of Damballah, undoubtedly—joining the other three.

While I beheld that mind-boggling sight, Uncle Ohisver got closer to me and placed his hand on my shoulder.

"I'm glad fate has given me this opportunity to see you again, Hugo," he said. "My time has come, but I leave happier knowing that you're carrying on our tradition."

Meanwhile, inside the vortex, the Gods conversed and possibly clashed. I was looking at an unfathomable sight, beyond human comprehension. I also saw the agitated silhouettes of Legendre, Marie, Ascension, Zaka and Zigor, but couldn't guess what was going on.

I'll never knew if it was an illusion, or an effect of being so close to the godly vortex, but I was at last able to clearly see the forms of the *loa* that spiraled all around us like pale butterflies caught in a whirlpool of energy.

Behind my uncle Ohisver, I suddenly began to observe other, ghostly forms: those of the Van Helsings of the past, stretching back into history. They were all here: Gideon and his daughter Talia, Ithamar, Tivel, Aharon and Kappel, the ancestor, the first of the American Van Helsings.

Ohisver's body was surrounded by the *loa*, who began to cling to him like barnacles on a ship. As more and more of the Voodoo spirits gathered around him, his figure started to become translucent, ethereal, until he finally disappeared into the light. He had gone to join his ancestors as I would, one day, join mine.

Suddenly, there was an explosion of radiance, a silent thunderclap, a supernatural outburst that assaulted the mind, rather than the human senses.

The Gods vanished.

All the zombies crumbled, fell apart, began to turn into nauseating piles of dust.

Where the vortex had been mere seconds earlier, there were now only five, small human figures—no, only three, for two—Zaka and Marie—appeared consumed from the inside, as if time and the normal order of nature had suddenly reasserted its power. Their bodies turned to smoke, than quickly dissipated in the wind, more real than a cloud, yet less material than a phantasm. In a matter of seconds, it was as if they had never been there at all.

Legendre, Ascension and Zigor fell to the ground, like puppets whose strings had just been cut.

Dawn had begun to appear over the horizon. A pale, wan light soon bathed the terrace. The stench of the zombie dust was replaced by a strange fragrance, not unlike the smell of vanilla.

I rushed towards the three forms that lay on the ground. A mere glance was enough to verify that Legendre would never again bother anyone. Jonathan's bullets had, at last, done their work. The evil *houngan* was well and truly dead, half of his head still missing. His eloquence had obviously failed to sway the Gods to his mad, grandiose plans...

I saw the Key of Sakbata crumble into dust, soon followed by the Dagger of Hevioso and the Cup of Erzulie, which both succumbed to an all-devouring rust. I understood the message that the Gods were sending us: *"Don't call us, we'll call you."*

I helped Ascension get back to her feet. My young cousin seemed unscathed. Then, it was Zigor's turn. I became curious when I noticed that the Medallion of Damballah now hung around his neck. And even though he was still a zombie, somehow he looked different.

I sniffed the air. He no longer carried with him the stench of the living dead. His eyes were less vitreous than before. Could it be that...?

"Damballah's parting gift," muttered Zigor, rubbing the Medallion between his fingers. "A damn fine idea he had..."

Could it be that...?

Wednesday, August 31

THE HOUSE WAS IN GOOD HANDS.

I handed the keys of Saint-Amadou over to Ascension.

"You'll come back soon?" she asked.

I shook my head. I honestly didn't know when I would be able to return to New Orleans. The Club business did not leave me much time for family gatherings. But I left the city with a serene heart. I had made peace with my uncle and my past, and would no longer be haunted by the regrets of having disappointed him and failed in my duties.

The inheritance of the American Van Helsings was safe with Ascension. Probably safer than with me. She would be the one entrusted with the duty of watching over Saint-Amadou and its occult secrets. I doubted there was a sorcerer alive who could take her—or even a God. Yes, Uncle Ohisver would be happy, I thought. The House was in good hands.

"I'll do everything in my power to be back for Mardi-Gras," I said finally, giving her a kiss. And I was sincere when I said it. I would.

It had taken a full day for Zigor to return to normal. I documented his reverse transformation, from zombie back to human, with photos, temperature charts, blood and DNA samples. It was probably the first time in history that a zombie had ever become human again. Once it had all been analyzed, I was planning to have a serious conversation with my Hunter Tatiana Dovchenko, who still had some connections at Biopreparat, the former Soviet Union's top secret bacteriological war lab.

Zigor reverted to being the same good old Zigor I knew and loved, except that he had few fragmented memories of the events of the night before. My theory was that, as his brain had regenerated, it had rebooted to its former state and deleted most of the new information he had acquired during the Judgment of the Masks.

We would likely not find out anything more from him about the Savanna and the Great Beyond, and it was probably better that way.

One thing was new though: Zigor now wore the Medallion of Damballah on a chain around his neck under his shirt, for he was now the Earthly incarnation of the Father of Serpents and Master of the *loa*—something that would not handicap him too much, I suspected, in his job as a criminal defense attorney. Ascension and I had discussed the possibility that Zigor was obliged to keep wearing the Medallion to prevent him from becoming a zombie again. We could have tried to test our theory by trying to take it away, but Zigor wasn't keen on the idea, and personally, I would not recommend that anyone try to separate an incarnation from his talisman by force. Things could get very ugly very quickly...

Before leaving Saint-Amadou, I briefed Zigor on what had happened during the night of the Judgment of Masks, including the unhappy disappearance of Jonathan Hamilton, gone missing in action, probably killed by one of Legendre's zombies. I had conducted a cursory search of Marie's property before leaving, but hadn't found any trace of his body.

That was when Zigor made what may have been his greatest revelation: it was Jonathan who had killed him the previous Saturday night!

Yes, it was Jonathan who had almost decapitated him with a machete to incriminate Legendre, before stabbing himself in the right shoulder to divert our suspicions—not that we had had any.

He explained that Jonathan had been pushed into killing him that night because, during his Internet investigation, he had just stumbled upon the fact that there never was and never had been a law firm called Hamilton & Hamilton in New Orleans.

In other words, *Jonathan Hamilton did not exist.*

And neither did his father, who was not one of Frank Clayton's victims, as we had all been led to believe. The office on St. Charles was a recent lease, too.

Thanks to James Citrin, who had finally come through with some useful tidbits, Zigor had discovered that everything the young man had told us was a lie, a fabrication, a mendacious manipulation of which we had become the gullible victims.

Further research showed that behind Hamilton & Hamilton, SIMBI and Legendre's Haitian-American Development Corporation was a shadowy corporate entity called BlackSpear Holdings, but there, all the trails stopped. Even Citrin was unable, or perhaps unwilling, to tell us more.

BlackSpear had manipulated Clayton to kill my uncle. They had used Legendre to destroy the city and, through Jonathan, had succeeded in getting me and my friends to rid them of the compromising and potentially dangerous Haitian.

Why? What were the sinister motives behind the conspiracy? With Jonathan dead or gone, it was unlikely that we would ever find out the truth.

As was often the case with real life, the mystery would remain unsolved.

I sat behind the wheel of my old Dodge. Zigor took the passenger seat next to me, often dubbed the "dead man's seat," which gave us both a good chuckle, considering the situation. It's in moments like that that having a zombie for a traveling companion can really relieve the boredom of a long road trip.

We left New Orleans to its looters and desperate citizens, fighting for survival.

It had only been the day before that the Government had finally begun to take action to rescue New Orleans. Eighty-five percent of the city was still underwater. Thousands of people were without food and water. The failure of the authorities to act was inconceivable and would remain so to me for a long time to come, perhaps forever.

Later, I discovered that it was thought 3000 people had died because of Katrina, and 700 vanished, their bodies never to be found. Legendre could probably have told the authorities where they were, but he, too, was gone without a trace. The evil *houngan* who had caused this catastrophe was now merely another shadow amongst the shadows that would haunt New Orleans forever. Two hundred fifty thousand people had left the city, forcibly relocated or exiled with no hope of ever returning... Some even said that that figure might, in time, grow to reach a million...

But none of that was anything I could change.

Thursday, September 1

ANOTHER DAY AND WE MIGHT HAVE LOST ALL CREDIBILITY.

The office of the Vice President of the United States is located, as everyone now knows since the eponymous television series, in the famous West Wing of the White House.

The current occupant had it redecorated to look like a serious, sober, almost austere, sanctum, more likely to evoke an atmosphere of state secrets and hard sweat and labor than one of diplomatic ceremonials and pointless receptions. A man-sized safe occupied an entire corner of the room. On the wall behind the Vice President's desk was an old map of the country's Eastern Seaboard. The desk itself, made of black teak, was permanently buried under files and lit up by a single desk lamp with a pale shade.

The White House rules normally required that the names of every visitor to this eminent office, and the minutes of every meeting held therein, be logged in and recorded by the Secret Service—whether they were foreign dignitaries or Boy Scout leaders. But the Vice President, who had a deep aversion to sharing his secrets with the rest of the world, had, since his swearing in, and in the all-powerful name of security, found ways to circumvent these rules.

Therefore, the names of the two men who were introduced that afternoon into his office never appeared on any official records of the U.S. Government. If, in the future, some curious historian, surprised to not find a copy of the Vice President's agenda in the National Archives, was nevertheless successful in locating it, he would learn only that, on September 1 2005, at 4 p.m., the Vice President had received two delegates from the Montana Chamber of Commerce and Agriculture who had come to discuss the use of hormones and antibiotics in cattle raising. Nothing really out of the ordinary.

"Please take a seat," said the Vice President to the two men, who had nothing to do with either Montana or cattle raising. "Did you have a good trip?" he barked in his usually brusque manner.

"Excellent, thank you, Mr. Vice President," replied Count Corona.

He was a man in his early 60s, of medium size, impeccably manicured with stylish silver hair. He wore a genuine bespoke Savile Row suit and spoke English with barely a nuance of Mid-Atlantic accent which might have betrayed his European origins.

"Thank you for seeing us so promptly, Dick," said Prescott Brown.

The man from the Clock Company was in his 50s, tall, lanky, refined, with a misleadingly open and friendly face. He was dressed conservatively, with discreet elegance. His voice marked him as a man belonging to the American elite, who had studied at Yale, made a fortune on Wall Street and retired to Martha's Vineyard.

"We agreed," said Corona, "to brief you in person as soon as the Katrina Protocol had been effected."

"And not a moment too soon either," grumbled the Vice President. "Our inaction of the last few days might cost us dearly, politically I mean. Another day and we might have lost all credibility."

"It's not that bad," said Brown, smiling. "The American people have short memories, and your friends in the media will provide you with cover as usual. I saw on TV yesterday that the President had flown over New Orleans. An excellent idea; very good move. It'll help his image."

"Harumph," grumbled the Vice President. "So we're done?"

"Yes," said Corona. "To borrow a phrase, 'Mission Accomplished.' We have reached our objectives. The goals we sought are now within our grasp and the changes we have achieved are irreversible. Our respective organizations, BlackSpear Holdings and the Clock Company, are very pleased with the results of the Protocol. Your administration now has a completely free hand in Louisiana and much can be done there."

"Good," said the Vice President. "I'll brief the President myself tomorrow. Now that the job is done, I'll tell FEMA to move ahead with the rescue efforts."

"You can, of course, count on us for further assistance, if you need it," said Corona.

"Ditto with the Clock Company," said Brown.

A silence full of momentous, yet unsaid words followed

"The results were worth the gamble, Mr. Vice President," said Corona, who felt that the politician before him was still debating the costs of the operation. "As you know, the Port of New Orleans is one of America's most important harbors, through which most of your grain exports and petroleum imports transit. Thanks to the Protocol, BlackSpear and its subsidiaries will be ideally positioned to win the future contracts for its reconstruction. There are billions to be made, of which naturally your party and your former employer will see their share."

"New Orleans was in the grip of the Democrats," added Brown. "As long as it was in the hands of *those people*, there was nothing you could do. Now that it's been cleansed of its undesirables, the tide will turn in your favor. Once the clean-up is over, the city will become gentrified, just as Charleston did after Hurricane Hugo. Its new residents will vote Republican. Louisiana will tip over to your side."

"We'll make sure that the insurance companies either delay or refuse payments," said Corona. "The poorer residents will be economically forced to move..."

"Yes. We've already planned for relocation camps in Texas and other sites are under construction," said the Vice President.

"Excellent!" said Brown. "We'll soon be buying up as much real estate as we can, when the prices hit bottom, of course. In ten years, New Orleans will be a new Houston."

"According to our estimates," said Corona, "there's a trillion dollars to be made in the ethnic cleansing of the city."

"You are a great statesman, Dick!"

"And there are no concerns to be had from... Voodoo?" asked the Vice President, uttering that last word with undisguised disgust.

"None at all," said Corona, emphatically. "The Haitian whom we used to reach our objectives was eliminated. All trails leading back to BlackSpear have also been severed. As my ancestors used to say, one must always *cut off the branch*. The images of looting and violence broadcast 24/7 by the media have further made credible the intervention of private security forces on US soil to restore order. They have enabled us to further control the information and eliminate any possibilities of... leaks."

"An excellent rehearsal for the future, if we ever get to that point," said Brown.

"I'm proud to say that it was my own son who personally oversaw the Katrina Protocol from beginning to end, and gave us this great victory," said Corona.

That same day, at about the same time, a young man whom we know as Jonathan Hamilton, but whose real identity was Carlo, Viscount Corona, drove onto a small private airstrip located barely 40 miles outside of New Orleans, the existence of which was not mentioned on any official maps.

As planned, a Learjet 45, marked with the logo of BlackSpear Holdings, a black circle crossed diagonally by a white line, was waiting for him.

Ten minutes later, after a brief chat with the pilot, Carlo Corona took off.

The old Dodge Charger '68 with Hugo Van Helsing at the wheel was driving west along Route 90 towards Texas, leaving Louisiana behind. In its front passenger seat, Zigor Side looked at the perfectly blue, totally cloudless sky.

Katrina had come and gone, leaving behind a grim cortege of death and destruction. If it were not for the heaps of debris littering the road and the countryside, no one could have suspected the nightmarish reality of the last few days.

Hugo had turned on the radio, desperately looking for a station that wasn't talking about the hurricane 24/7. Turning the dial at random, he had eventually found KCOL 92.5 FM, which broadcast golden oldies from

Groves, Texas: Paul McCartney, Lionel Ritchie, Elton John... As the years went by, the notion of "golden oldies" had progressively shifted from '50s rock to '70s.

Zigor noticed a small silver dot, high in the azure sky.

He put his hand on the Medallion of Damballah which hung on his chest under his open neck shirt. The Medallion which he would be forced to wear for... For how long exactly, he wondered? Eternity might be a long time...

He looked again the silver dot which moved slowly against the sky and smiled.

But there are compensations, he thought.

Aboard the Learjet, Carlo Corona had just finished adding a few extra notes to his report on the Katrina Protocol on his laptop—in particular, a directive recommending the elimination of Hugo Van Helsing, who might some day prove a danger to the Society.

He was about to press the *send* button, which would instantaneously transmit his report to BlackSpear's headquarters, where his father would find it when he returned from Washington, when he suddenly heard a noise behind him.

That was impossible. He knew that there was no one but he and the pilot in the plane currently flying at 50,000 feet.

He turned around.

He noticed at once that the air had acquired a strange density, almost viscous, *liquid*.

Then, a shape began to form.

Before him stood a hideous zombie which, quick as lightning, lunged forward and hungrily plunged its razor-sharp teeth deep into the young man's neck.

Carlo Corona did not even have time to scream before he died.

An hour later, when the Learjet landed at another private airstrip near Houston, the pilot and the ground crew discovered the untouched body of Carlo Corona, who appeared to have died from fright, even though no one could have entered or escaped from the plane.

No one human, anyway.

From the Diaries of Hugo Van Helsing

Taken by, taken by the sky
Dreams unwind and love's a state of mind...
Fleetwood Mac had just finished playing *Rhiannon* on the radio when the road sign indicated that we were leaving Cameron Parish, the last Parish of Louisiana, to enter Orange County, the first County of Texas.

To my right, Zigor had his eyes closed, looking relaxed in his seat. I could tell that he wasn't sleeping, because his head was gently swinging back and forth in time to the music. With his left hand, he was slowly rubbing the Medallion of Damballah, almost as if he were trying to polish it.

He was smiling.

I wondered what he was thinking about.

"What didn't go right?"
President George W. Bush, in a remarkable moment of candor, quoted by House Minority Leader Nancy Pelosi, after she urged him to fire FEMA Director Michael Brown "because of all that went wrong, of all that didn't go right" in the Katrina relief effort. [4]

While thousands of Mississippians who lost their homes to Hurricane Katrina remain in FEMA trailers, the federal government on Friday approved a state plan to spend $600 million in grants earmarked for housing on a major expansion of the state-owned port—a project that could eventually include casino and resort facilities.

Mike Stuckey
Senior news editor, MSNBC
January 25, 2008

---

[4] Source: USATODAY, 9/7/2005.

Tales of Club Van Helsing

The Lying Dutchmen

The American Van Helsings
The Secret History of America's most Gothic Family
by George Stark
(Miskatonic University Press, 1997) [5]

The patriarch and founding father of the American branch of the Van Helsings was **Kapel Van Helsing** (1594-1644). Kapel left Holland to seek his fortune in the New World at age 20. He was accompanied by his young wife, Dana Loewe, the daughter of the rabbi of Utrecht. Kapel and Dana had three children: Hadar, a daughter, born in 1615, and two sons, Harel, born in 1620, and Izak, born in 1630.

In 1624, Kapel Van Helsing distinguished himself by becoming one of the founders of the Dutch colony of Nieuw Amsterdam, which was rechristened New York in 1665. During the years that followed, he worked closely with Peter Minuit, the Colony's director-general, and was involved in the purchase of the island of Manhattan from the native tribe, the Canarsee. In 1626, Hadar died during a cholera epidemic. In 1628, Kapel

---

[5] An essay in creative mythography.

Van Helsing founded the Amsterdammer Club, which still exists today. Tragically, his relationship with the local tribes grew worse over the years and, in 1640, he found himself in conflict with the Muh-he-ka-ne-ok (Mohicans) from Conyne Eylandt (Coney Island), a place dubbed *Narrioch*, the *shadowless land*, by the natives. During the ensuing battle, the intervention of the Bear-God Mahkwa caused the death of Dana and Harel. Even though he emerged victorious, Kapel Van Helsing was never able to recover from such a tragic loss. Four years later, he died at age 50. He was buried in the Van Helsing crypt, located under the Amsterdammer Club.

Kapel's sole surviving son, **Izak Van Helsing** (1630-1685), decided to leave Nieuw Amsterdam after his father's death. In 1644, at age 14, he joined the crew of the schooner *Prinz Willem* as a cabin boy. We then lose all traces of him until 1661, when he is mentioned as the secret lover of Robin Whitby, the famous captain of *Neptune's Lady*, a woman who passed herself off as a man. It would seem that Robin gave Izak a son, Raziel Van Helsing, born in 1662. Later, Izak Van Helsing became captain of the *Sémillante* and teamed up with the female pirate known as *Bouche Rouge* (Scarlet Lips) to attack Spanish galleons. Izak Van Helsing died in 1685, fighting alongside Captain Blood in the Caribbean.

Raziel Van Helsing (1662-1699) grew up on Tortuga Island, located on the northern coast of Haiti. In 1680, he was an established trader at Cap Français (today's Cap Haïtien). In 1681, he met Catherine Monvoisin, a.k.a. La Voisin, the infamous adventuress who had been condemned to death in France during the "Poison Affair," but had secretly escaped the gallows by trading her silence against a reduced sentence of lifelong exile. In 1682, Raziel Van Helsing and La Voisin had a son, Jeremiah; then, in 1684, a daughter, Hadar. No one knows why, but in 1690, Raziel left Haiti, taking only Jeremiah with him, and returned to New York, where he renewed his family's acquaintance with the Amsterdammer Club. The ultimate fates of La Voisin and Hadar remain, to date, a complete mystery. In 1691, Raziel Van Helsing supported Jacob Leisler's doomed rebellion, but managed to avoid being hanged. In 1692, he married Laurel Doone with whom, three years later, he had a daughter, Mazhira. In 1699, at age 37, Raziel Van Helsing went to sea with his friend, the British Doctor Lemuel Gulliver, and never returned.

Jeremiah Van Helsing (1682-1719), the son of Raziel Van Helsing and La Voisin, became the archenemy of the necromancer James Boon who, in 1710, had founded the town of Jerusalem's Lot in the State of Maine. The details of the conflict that pit Raziel against Boon remain obscure, but we do know that the young Van Helsing managed to wrest away the sorcerer's own granddaughter, Ann, whom he married in 1711. That same year, they had a son, Yakob. Two years later, Jeremiah Van Helsing met an even deadlier threat: that of Joseph Curwen, the infamous warlock of Providence, Rhode Island. Jeremiah Van Helsing was murdered by Curwen in 1719 and died at the same age as his father—37.

Meanwhile, **Mazhira Van Helsing** (1695-1729), the daughter of Raziel Van Helsing and Laurel Doone, married Daniel Bummpo in 1715. She had two children: Abigail in 1717 and Nathaniel (a.k.a. Natty) in 1719. Unfortunately, Daniel, Mazhira and Abigail were killed by the Mohicans in 1729.

Yakob Van Helsing (1711-1758), Jeremiah's son, continued his father's battle against Joseph Curwen.

They reached a stalemate in 1734. In 1735, Yakob Van Helsing married Cassandra Warren, the granddaughter of the notorious witch Melinda Warren. They had three children: Gideon, born in 1736, Odelia, born in 1738, and Chana, born in 1739. In 1746, after another hopeless fight with Curwen, during which young Odelia lost her life, Yakob Van Helsing and his family were forced to flee New York and find refuge in their ancestral home in Cap Français in Haiti. In 1751, Yakob Van Helsing was initiated into the Voodoo religion and became a respected *houngan*. Some say that this is when the Van Helsings first met Marie Laveau. He later supported a slave revolt organized by the *houngan* François Mackandal and fought alongside him from 1752 to 1758. Sadly, Mackandal was betrayed, captured and burned alive by the French at Cap Français in 1758. Yakob Van Helsing and his family were also executed.

Gideon Van Helsing (1736-1787) had already left Haiti at age 18 to sail with freebooters when his family was killed by the French. In 1760, he teamed up with the pirate Long John Silver, before finding himself in New Orleans. There, he had a *liaison* with "Madame Minuit," a famous *mambo*, with whom he had a daughter, Talia. But Gideon Van Helsing was still pursued by the King's Justice for his father's "crimes" and his own acts of piracy against the French, so he had to flee Louisiana. In 1767, he appeared in Kentucky, working alongside Daniel Boone. In 1771, he traveled to Providence, challenged Joseph Curwen to a sorcerous duel and killed him, thereby avenging the murders of his ancestors. Gideon Van Helsing died in 1787 at age 51 in the town of Sleepy Hollow, after having tried to tackle the grim specter of the Headless Horseman.

Gideon's daughter, **Talia Van Helsing** (1761-1815), grew up in New Orleans, was initiated into the Voodoo rites by her mother and thus became a famous *mambo*. On March 21, 1782, at age 21, she fought off the evil *Boum'ba Maza*, which caused a fire that almost destroyed the city. Two years later, Talia Van Helsing married Robert Carter, a gentleman from Virginia, with whom she had two sons: John in 1785 and Ithamar after her separation in 1786, when she reverted to using her maiden name for both herself and him. In 1815, Talia Van Helsing died at age 54 during the Battle of New Orleans.

Talia's son, **Ithamar Van Helsing** (1786-1841), left New Orleans at age 18 to accompany Lewis and Clark on their famous expedition. Some claim that, while in Montana, he fell in love and married a native lycanthrope with whom he had a son, Tivel. In 1815, back in New Orleans, Ithamar Van Helsing fought valiantly alongside Jean Lafitte during the Battle of New Orleans, but could not prevent his mother's death. The following year, he began construction on Saint-Amadou, which was to become the Van Helsings' house in New Orleans. In March 1828, Ithamar Van Helsing defeated Captain Obed Marsh's Esoteric Order of Dagon, which was trying to gain a foothold in Louisiana. In February 1836, with Davy Crockett's help, Ithamar Van Helsing managed to prevent the Smoking Mirror of Quetzalcoatl from falling into the clutches of Mexican General Santa Anna, who had besieged the Alamo where the Mirror was hidden. In January 1841, at age 55, Ithamar Van Helsing was murdered by P.T. Barnum during the production of his *Greatest Show on Earth* in New Orleans.

Tivel Van Helsing (1806-1865), Ithamar's son, like many of his ancestors, yielded to the call of the sea and, at age 14 joined the crew of Captain Ahab's *Pequod* as a cabin boy. Back in Nantucket, he befriended young Arthur Gordon Pym and almost embarked with him on the *Grampus* in 1827. He was prevented from doing so by having to do battle with the Esoteric Order of Dagon in nearby Innsmouth. Tivel Van Helsing was eventually rescued by his father and brought back to New Orleans. Two years later, he married a local witch, Rosalie Mayfair, with whom he had two children: Aharon, born in 1829, and Danya, born in 1831. Danya kept her mother's name and, in 1859, gave birth to Andrew Blodgett Mayfair, Sr. In 1836, Tivel Van Helsing renewed his acquaintance with Arthur Gordon Pym, who had just returned from Antarctica. No one knows what transpired between the two, but it is considered very likely that the two men played a part in the mysterious death of journalist Edgar Allan Poe in 1849. Tivel Van Helsing's activities during the Civil War remain a mystery. It seems that he was implicated in the assassination of Abraham Lincoln on April 16, 1865, at the behest of the Amsterdammer Club and the Gun Club. Tivel Van Helsing was murdered a few days later, probably to secure his silence.

Aharon Van Helsing (1829-1899) left New Orleans in 1847 at age 18. He traveled to Holland to study and meet his cousin, Abraham Van Helsing, who was the same age as he and with whom he had been corresponding. The two Van Helsings then traveled throughout Europe. In 1852 in Rome, Aharon Van Helsing fell in love with the granddaughter of the 15th Phantom, Maria Walker, and married her the following year. In 1854, they had a son, Malachi. For the next ten years, the couple traveled with Captain Nemo aboard the *Nautilus*, before eventually returning to New Orleans in

1865, just after Tivel's death. In the years that followed, Aharon Van Helsing battled Doctor Miguelito Loveless, met Mark Twain, fought a duel with Rhett Butler and, to redeem his father's reputation for the part he had played in Lincoln's assassination, challenged P.T. Barnum. In particular, Tivel Van Helsing helped Oscar Zoroaster Diggs to escape Barnum's wrath by fleeing in a hot air balloon that took the would-be "Wizard" to the Land of Oz. In 1868, Aharon and Maria Van Helsing, besieged by Barnum's forces, were forced to flee New Orleans and, in a repeat of history, find refuge in their ancestral home in Haiti. Aharon's only visit to the United States after that was a brief stop in Virginia to celebrate the birth of his cousin, Randolph Carter. In April 1876, Aharon Van Helsing took part in the uprising that overthrew Haitian President Michel Domingue and his henchman, the British strangler, Mayes. Aharon Van Helsing died in his bed at age 70.

Malachi Van Helsing (1854-1912) grew up in Haiti. Then, according to files kept by Morrison, Morrison & Dodd, he was employed by the New Orleans branch of the Netherland-Sumatra Company in 1875 and was involved in the "Giant Rat" Affair. In August 1876, Malachi Van Helsing was in Deadwood, South Dakota, when Wild Bill Hicock was shot. In 1891-92, he helped John Reid in his fight against the Black Arrow. In 1898, he visited the Klondike where he befriended Jack London and found gold. Wealthy and semi-retired, Malachi Van Helsing returned to New Orleans in 1900 and had an affair with the notorious adventuress Josephine Balsamo, with whom he had a son, Ruven. In 1906, Malachi Van Helsing was in San Francisco just before the famous earthquake that almost destroyed the city. In 1907, he returned to Haiti, where he met Doctor Jules de

Grandin. In 1908, Malachi Van Helsing joined Professor Challenger and Lord Roxton on a South American expedition. In 1909, he met Sigmund Freud and Carl Jung during their American visit. Malachi Van Helsing died aboard the *Titanic* in 1912, at age 58.

Ruven Van Helsing (1901-1951), Malachi's son, joined young Doctor Francis Ardan in 1925 on a polar expedition that unearthed a "thing" from another world. Four years later, he and the Amsterdammer Club were accused of a complicated stock fraud, but never charged. Right after "Black Tuesday" (October 29, 1929), Ruven Van Helsing joined Professor Littlejohn on his expedition to the so-called "Mountains of Madness" in Antarctica. When he returned, in March 1930, he established residence in Hollywood, where he began to socialize with film celebrities. There, Ruven Van Helsing married a young actress, Olga Krichnoff, with whom he had a son, Ohisver. Tragically, Olga was kidnapped by Barnum and became the victim of a monstrous experiment which was said to have inspired the ending of the movie *Freaks*, made the following year by one of Ruven's friends, director Tod Browning. Olga survived for only two years and many suspect that her husband deliberately put an end to her miserable life. In 1934, Ruven Van Helsing returned to New Orleans, where he had to fight the *houngan* Rodil Mocquino, who had taken over Saint-Amadou. In 1941, he returned to Hollywood where he and Orson Welles battled Doctor Saturday. After World War II, Ruven Van Helsing alternated between spending time in New Orleans, where he lived with Carême Proudfoot, and in Haiti, where he was sometimes known as "Reverend Van Helsing." Ruven Van Helsing was murdered in 1951 in his house at Cap Haitien by the evil *houngan* Buonaparte Gallia.

Ohisver Van Helsing (1932-2005) accompanied Jack Kerouac and Neal Cassady during their 1947 travels through America, and Che Guevara during his 1952 motorbike journey in South America. There, he met Father Rodin of the Jesuits. In 1953, he introduced his half-sister, the daughter of Carême Proudfoot, to Marie Laveau in order for the girl to be initiated into the rites of Voodoo. Later, Ohisver Van Helsing assisted the Shop during their clean-up operations in Mill Valley, California. During the next ten years, Ohisver traveled throughout North and South America. He was in Haiti in 1957, where he met Zaka and the *houngan* Soulagé Minfort. In 1965, he offered his hospitality to Patience Latrelle, the daughter of Buonaparte Gallia and Simone Latrelle. In 1968, he was involved in the 300 million yen robbery in Tokyo. In 1970, he helped Barnabas Collins in his battle against the monstrous Leviathans. In 1973, he befriended Voodoo experts Doctor Jericho Drumm and Marie-Juliette Edmonds. With no known heirs, Ohisver Van Helsing concentrated his efforts on the education of the youngest descendent of the European branch of the Van Helsings, Hugo Van Helsing. After 1995, Ohisver Van Helsing retired from business and became a virtual recluse in Saint-Amadou. He died in a public shooting in 2005.

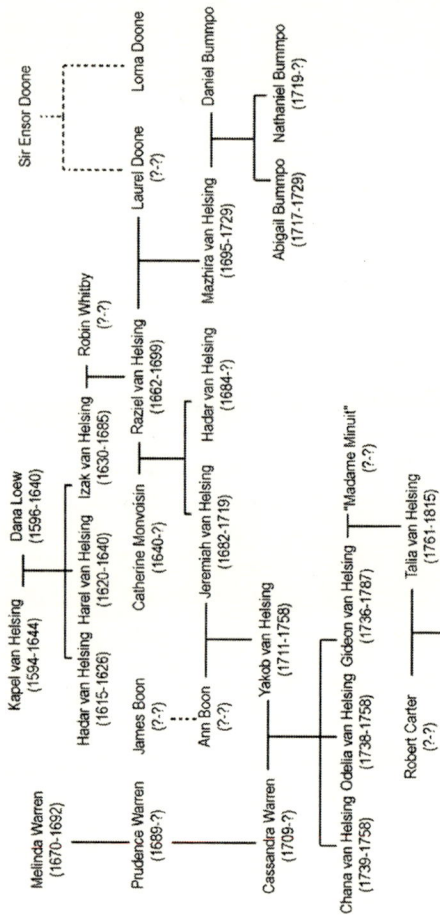

Sir Ensor Doone

Laurel Doone
(?-?)

Lorna Doone

Kapel van Helsing
(1594-1644)

Dana Loew
(1596-1640)

Izak van Helsing
(1630-1685)

Robin Whitby
(?-?)

Mazhira van Helsing
(1695-1729)

Daniel Bummpo

Hadar van Helsing
(1615-1626)

Harel van Helsing
(1620-1640)

Catherine Monvoisin
(1640-?)

Raziel van Helsing
(1662-1699)

Hadar van Helsing
(1684-?)

Abigail Bummpo
(1717-1729)

Nathaniel Bummpo
(1719-?)

James Boon
(?-?)

Ann Boon
(?-?)

Jeremiah van Helsing
(1682-1719)

Melinda Warren
(1670-1692)

Prudence Warren
(1689-?)

Yakob van Helsing
(1711-1758)

Gideon van Helsing
(1736-1787)

"Madame Minuit"
(?-?)

Cassandra Warren
(1709-?)

Chana van Helsing
(1739-1758)

Odelia van Helsing
(1738-1758)

Talia van Helsing
(1761-1815)

Robert Carter
(?-?)

PAGE 2

168

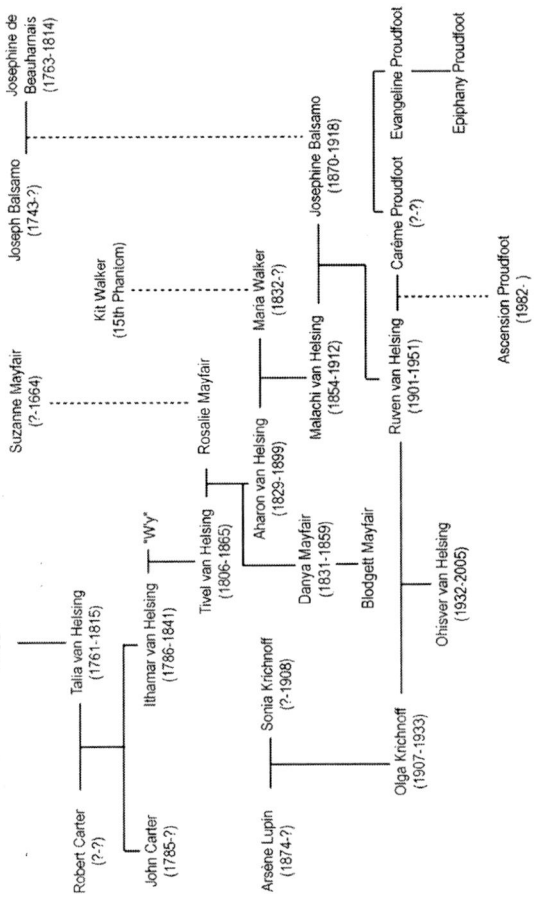

The Clay Dogs

to Philippe Xavier

"Marie, please tell me a story!"

Marie Laveau looked at young Hugo Van Helsing. The rambunctious eight-year-old liked to come to play in the vast shady park of her mansion in Bayou St. John, and his uncle Ohisver was happy to let him enjoy the company of the great *mambo*. After a few hours spent running and hiding amongst the majestic cypresses encrusted with Spanish moss, Hugo would generally retreat from the sweltering heat and humidity and rush back inside the house, to enjoy its refreshing coolness. There, he would while away the rest of the afternoon reading *Doctor Strange* comics or listening to Marie's stories.

Marie, whom some still called the "Voodoo Queen of New Orleans," liked the boy. She had immediately detected great potential in him and had used her wiles to persuade Ohisver to entrust part of his education to her. She hadn't had to argue much. She knew that, properly raised, young Hugo might grow up to become a great *houngan*, one who, one day, could tip the scales in the eternal combat.

"Marie, please tell me a story!" repeated the boy.

The *mambo* smiled.

"What kind of story would you like today, Hugo?" she asked.

"Something with lots of black magic," he replied enthusiastically, still clutching one of his favorite *Doctor Strange* comics.

"Show me," said Marie, gesturing for Hugo to give her the book.

"This is the one where Doc fights Dormammu after he's returned to the Dark Dimension and Umar..."

"I see. Well, would you like me to tell you about another man who was also a great and wise magician, who fought evil in all its guises?"

"Yes, please! Was he a superhero?"

"After a fashion, I suppose. His name was *houngan* Temu... Do you know what a *houngan* was?"

"No."

"A *houngan* was many things in those days: a justice of the peace, a law-giver, a cop on the beat, if you will, endowed with great magical powers."

"Cool."

"This story takes place a long, long time ago, thousands of years ago, in Africa. Not the poor and wretched continent that we know today, but a mighty land, proud and powerful, home to vast empires which are less than dust today. One of these Empires was that of the Dogon, a wonderful people who lived in Western Africa. It was ruled by the wise Lébé Serou from his capital of Ife, which is remembered today by less than a handful of men. Keeping the peace throughout the Empire were the *houngans*, a group of learned and powerful beings who..."

"Like the *Green Lantern Corps*, you mean?" interrupted Hugo.

Marie smiled. She had seen his comic book collection and understood the reference.

171

"Yes, like the *Green Lantern Corps*," she nodded. "And Temu, the man whose story I'm about to tell you, was the wisest and kindest of all the *houngans*." She smiled wistfully. "Now sit down and listen..."

Houngan *Temu and the Clay Dogs*

Once upon a time, *began Marie, houngan* Temu was returning from a long journey beyond the great savanna that lay east of the Empire's farthest border. What he had done there is a tale for another day. Suffice it to say that he and his great mount and companion, Agna, were tired, hungry and thirsty.

"Praise Amma! We have finally crossed the desert," said Temu, as he spied the village of Dogul. "There we shall find food and water."

Dogul was one of the poor settlements which eked a meager subsistence from the waters of the Nyambeenge River, whose periodic floods helped keep the local fields fertile. It consisted of no more than 30 houses made of mud and brick, encircled by a semi-fortified wall that had seen better days.

"Yes, I know you've done all the work, Agna, and I'm grateful," continued Temu, speaking to his mount. "But think, our long journey is almost over and soon we'll again see my brother!"

Now, you may think that the *houngan* was addressing his beast in the way we talk to horses and dogs. Not so! In those days, other species shared the land with the sons of man. One of these was the *tô*, great reptilian creatures who were gifted with intelligence and great sensitivity.

The village gates were open, as befitted this time of peace, so Temu rode through them. The rays of the sun were still beating down as mercilessly as ever, even though the afternoon was already half-over. As the *houngan* approached the town square, with its sacred baobab tree growing in the center, providing shade and comfort for all, he beheld an appalling sight. A group of villagers had gathered and begun to stone a half-naked man who lie at the foot of the tree, his blood staining the dirt.

"Stone him!" "Kill the *puru*!" screamed the crowd, *puru* meaning abomination.

The Emperor had long banished the practice of public stoning and Temu thought that the man must have been accused of some particularly abominable crime to provoke such anger. Note that I said "accused" and not "guilty," for he was a wise *houngan* and did not presume guilt on the basis of appearances alone.

"Stop!" he shouted, stepping into the middle of the crowd. In his right hand, he proudly held the intricately-carved staff that was both the vessel of a *houngan*'s power and an indication of his rank. The villagers immediately recognized him for who he was, and separated to let him pass. None wished to incur the wrath of a *houngan*, especially one as tall and powerful-looking as this one.

"What is going on? What has this man done?" inquired Temu in the sternest tone.

The villagers looked at each other, fearful of facing the penalties for having broken the Law of the Empire. Finally, one of them, either bolder or more foolish than the others, stepped out and confronted Temu.

"He is a murderer!" he said, pointing at the victim. "He killed our beloved *Olubaru*!" The Olubaru was the chief and the elder of the village. "He deserves to die!"

Some in the back of the crowd began barking, "Yes! Stone him! Kill him!"

Temu banged his staff on the ground and the shouts stopped at once.

"Silence! I am Temu, *houngan* of the Dogon. Has this man been properly judged, as prescribed by the laws of Lébé Serou?"

No one answered. They looked at each other, or at the ground, mute with shame and fear. As the realization of their guilt spread, some began to shuffle away meekly. Others, their heads bent down in sign of atonement, approached the *houngan* to place themselves at his disposal.

"Give some water and food to my *tô* and keep the accused under guard," ordered Temu. "I will conduct an inquiry into the crime according to the Law."

The man who had narrowly escaped being stoned to death stood up and wiped the blood from his arms and his face.

"Thank you, mighty *houngan*," he said. "My name is Kemenem. I am innocent."

"We shall see," said Temu. Then, he turned towards the villagers and asked: "Where is your *Baru*?" If the Olubaru is like the Mayor of a town, the *Baru* is like its Sheriff.

A man wearing the traditional green hat of the *Baru* stepped forward. He stood a good head taller than the other villagers. His face showed pride and determination. He, too, held a staff, although its carvings were fewer and less complex than Temu's.

"I am Ginu, *Baru* of Dogul," he said, introducing himself.

"And I, *houngan* Temu of the Dogon, Master of the Old Speech. I salute you, worthy Ginu." The two men exchanged a ritual salute, lowering their staffs and holding them parallel to the ground. Then Temu continued: "So you have found this man Kemenem to be guilty of murder?"

As two of the villagers took Kemenem away, and others were bringing a bucket of water for Temu's mount, the *houngan* and the *Baru* walked away from the square and into the narrow streets of the village.

"Kemenem is of the Binu Yoma clan," Ginu explained. "They hated the late *Olubaru* because they said that he cast a spell to entice the waters of the Nyambeenge to flow towards our fields, which they claim made their own fields barren... It is a lie, of course. We never took more water than the Law allows. It is not magic, but the Gods of the river who gave us more water. No one can say otherwise."

"I see," said Temu. "So you think that Kemenem came to kill your *Olubaru* to repay the harm he supposedly did to his clan?"

"Yes, I do."

"May I ask what other evidence you have?"

"After his wife found the *Olubaru*'s body," said Ginu, "we searched the house and found Kemenem hiding in a closet."

"A compelling case, it seems," said Temu, after a moment of reflection. The *houngan* then sensed an almost imperceptible easing in the *Baru*'s body. Ginu was trying to hide his relief from Temu, but had failed. The *houngan* thought that there was much here that remained hidden. So he said: "I would like to visit the home of the deceased." And at once, he sensed Ginu tensing again, confirming his suspicions.

"Very well. Follow me," said the *Baru*, barely concealing his displeasure.

They took a turn to the right and soon arrived before a house that was much larger than the others and more richly-decorated. Temu noticed the ceremonial markings above the threshold and nodded in approval. The *Olubaru* had obviously been a devout man, highly respectful of the Law of the Dogon, and had strictly followed all of the Emperor's orders.

Ginu knocked on the door. It soon opened, revealing a beautiful young woman dressed in a rich purple gown that made her look like the loveliest of orchids. Her eyes shone brightly, like black pearls. She wore the stone of widowhood on her forehead.

"This is Yapilu, the *Olubaru*'s widow," said Ginu. "Yapilu, this is *houngan* Temu."

"*Amma Inu*, Yapilu!" said Temu, bowing slightly.

"The *houngan* is investigating the death of your husband," explained Ginu once they had stepped inside. The air was fresh, smelling of rare perfumes. The walls has been painted white and the floor was stone-tiled, all signs of a modest but comfortable household.

The young woman's eyes betrayed her surprise. "But I thought that Kemenem had killed the *Olubaru*?" she said.

"I regret to inflict further pain on you, honorable Yapilu," said Temu, "but the Laws of Lébé Serou are clear. May I see the place where the noble *Olubaru*'s body was found?"

The young widow nodded and silently took them to a round adobe room decorated with many sacred paintings and carvings. On a shelf, next to a closet, were small jars, sculpted stones and a pile of scrolls and tablets. Several sacred masks stood on ornate stands, apparently undisturbed. At the center of the room was the traditional ritualistic brazier inside a tripod made of orichalc, and a small altar sculpted in a block of dark granite.

"This is where my husband worked his spells at night," explained Yapilu, somewhat unnecessarily.

Temu made a slow tour of the room, examining every item carefully. As he expected, there were no other entrances or exits, no windows, no skylights, not even a single crack in the wall. The *Olubaru* had been a most conscientious man.

"How did Kemenem get in?" he finally asked Yapilu.

"He'd come to beg my husband for work, and been allowed to stay on the property, in exchange for tending the gardens..."

"Obviously a pretext to do his dirty work," interrupted Ginu.

"The *Olubaru* was too generous," agreed Yapilu, with an undercurrent of raw emotion that Temu construed to be spite. "Kemenem slipped out of his shed last night, came into the house and killed the *Olubaru*. Then, when he heard me coming, he sought refuge in that closet where my husband kept his sacred herbs."

She pointed at the closet located next to the shelves. Its door, a simply decorated wood panel with an ordinary latch, was still half-open.

"I see," said Temu. Then, the *houngan* pointed his staff towards the three statuettes that stood on the altar next to the brazier.

"These clay dogs are?..."

"They are meant to draw the backlash of the spells cast by my husband," answered Yapilu.

"Ah yes. I am familiar with the practice." Temu raised his staff, clearly intending to smash the statuettes. "Let's see what magic the noble *Olubaru* has been casting recently..." Seeing Yapilu step back in panic, he added: "Have no fear. I am a *houngan*."

The staff hit the clay dogs. Small, white butterflies made of light briefly floated in the space over the broken statuettes, then, one by one, vanished. Temu watched them attentively. They did not convey a feeling of bad magic, only of good.

Then the *houngan* walked to the herb closet and pointed at the unlatched door.

"This is the closet where you found Kemenem?" he asked.

"Yes," said Yapilu. "I summoned Ginu immediately. Kemenem didn't have time to escape."

"He was inside? With the door locked?"

"Yes."

Temu made another tour of the room to give himself time to think, but he had seen enough.

"I would like to talk to Kemenem now," he said.

Ginu looked none too pleased, but went out and promptly returned with the accused in tow. Some salve had been used on his wounds and he was no longer bleeding. Temu instructed the man to sit down and began his interrogation by repeating the charges against him.

"Yes, it is true that our fields had grown fallow, and many of us blamed the *Olubaru*, but I did not," replied Kemenem. "When I came asking for work, he let me tend his garden and sleep in the shed outside. He was a kind and noble man. I grieve for his death as much as anyone else."

"What happened last night?" asked the *houngan*.

"I worked all day. The Sun was very hot. After Yapilu served dinner, I went back to my shed as I always do. I fell asleep, I did not go out. I don't know how I ended up in that closet, but I know I did not kill the *Olubaru*." Then, he repeated again, more forcefully: "He was a kind man!"

Temu stepped back and now addressed Ginu and Yapilu.

"When you want to cure a mad bull, seek the small thorn that drives him crazy," he began. "When seeking the truth of a murder, always search for the smallest *nyama*, for it is there that the greater evil hides..." A *nyama* is an evil stain, an ill-omened blot, a perfidious lie.

The *houngan* continued: "Ginu tried to hint at me that the *Olubaru* had cast black magic, yet none of the clay dogs showed any such thing. Yapilu accused Kemenem of having hidden in the closet after murdering her husband, a closet whose door, by her own admission, was locked, *even though it clearly locks only from the outside*."

The crestfallen faces of Ginu and Yapilu as they looked at the latch on the outside of the closet's paneled door was all the confession that any Imperial Magistrate would have required, but Temu relentlessly pursued his discourse.

"Since Kemenem could not have locked himself in, someone else had to do it, someone who had drugged his evening meal so that he would sleep and could be moved to the closet without awakening..." Then, the *houngan* directly confronted the two whom he had just accused of murder. "The *Olubaru* was old, and perhaps too generous with his wealth. You are both young and wanted him out of the way, but you had learned the lesson of the clay dogs. Someone else was needed to draw the backlash of your own evil actions. When Kemenem moved in, you saw the perfect opportunity and the deed was done."

Ginu had quickly recovered from the shock of having been so casually exposed. His hands gripped his staff tightly. *Too tightly*, thought Temu.

"An admirable deduction, worthy *houngan*; what do you intend to do now?" asked the *Baru*.

"The law of Lébé Serou is clear," replied Temu. "You and Yapilu will be taken to Ife to face the justice of the Emperor."

"I believe you have just returned from a long journey from the Lands Beyond?"

"That is true."

"So no one in Ife yet knows of your return?"

"Also true," said Temu, calmly. "Sadly, I have been unlucky in my efforts to communicate with the Empire."

"Then I can foresee a more pleasant alternative for Yapilu and me," said Ginu, grinning evilly.

The renegade *Baru* pointed his staff at Temu, murmuring some words in the Old Speech. A hideous, powerful *Ifrit* rose from within the wood and grew in size, until it loomed gigantically over the silent *houngan*, encircling the man's impassive form within its fleshy coils.

Temu, unfazed by the demon who was preparing to devour him, tapped his staff on the ground. An even greater *Ifrit* suddenly arose, a mighty horned beast bellowing as if all the circles of Hell itself could no longer hold him captive. Growing to truly colossal size, it briefly stood silhouetted against the evening sky, towering over the village itself. Then, swifter than the eyes could follow, it appeared to shrink and then swooped down, devouring Ginu's own demon, chewing it to pieces and swallowing it in a single, mighty gulp.

Then, the *Ifrit* turned towards the evil *Baru* and, almost as an afterthought, plucked him off the ground with its clawed hand as casually as a boy plucks a daisy from a field to hand to his girlfriend.

The *Baru*'s scream of horror and pain was soon cut short.

"Ginu!" cried Yapilu in anguish as she saw her lover being consumed by the demon.

His grisly task finished, the *Ifrit* evaporated into a foul-smelling miasmic cloud which coalesced around the *houngan*'s staff before being slowly reabsorbed into it.

"I am *houngan* Temu, Master of the Old Speech," said Temu to the few villagers who had dared enter the house. "This is the Law of the Dogon. I will appoint a new *Baru* and Yapilu will go to Ife to face the justice of the Dogon."

Temu stepped outside the house. Agna, his *tô*, was already waiting for him, having sensed that his master's business was done and that the time had come for them to depart. The *houngan* mounted his faithful companion and left Dogul, riding north.

"As for me, my road is still long before I gaze again upon the face of Emperor Lébé Serou—my brother."

Women, Fools and Serpents

"We should always deal cautiously with fire, water, women, fools, serpents and members of a royal family; for they may at once bring about our death."
Chanakya
(Indian politician, 350 BC-275 BC)

"I seek the human Van Helsing, who claims to be hunting monsters," said the Sea Serpent.

The creature had suddenly burst out of the water and towered over the ship, terrifying the sailors who were already signing themselves and confessing a vast litany of sins.

"Van Helsing, you say? Never heard the name," said Izak Van Helsing, Captain of the *Sémillante*, without losing his cool. He turned towards his second in command, first mate and not-so-secret lover, the beautiful Scarlet Lips. "Does that name ring a bell, darling?" he asked her

"I can't say that it does," replied the blonde woman.

"Sorry, can't help you there, mate," said Izak to the Serpent, flashing what he hoped would look like a convincingly sincere, warm smile.

"What a bother," said the Serpent. "If you could help me find that pesky mortal, I might be prepared to be generous..." The Monster tried, but utterly failed, to look sympathetic.

"Generous, how so? asked Izak Van Helsing, raising an eyebrow.

"I will promise you a quick and painless death instead of chewing on the marrow of your outer appendages," suggested the Serpent.

"A tempting offer, indeed, but I still find myself oddly unmotivated," said Izak Van Helsing. "Perhaps if I were to know more about your quest... Why exactly do you seek that Van...? Van...?"

"Van Helsing. It has come to my attention that that wretched little man has had the temerity to stalk some of this world's greatest denizens."

"Ah!—you mean Monsters."

"Watch your tongue, manling. I mean creatures such as me, who are ancient, learned and beautiful..."

"Sorry to interrupt," interjected Scarlet Lips, "but we've just met the Zombie King in Saint-Domingue and, Lord, he was *uuuugly*!"

"Well, perhaps not zombies then," said the Serpent.

"And what about that mangy Kroatoan wolf-monster, flea-ridden and slobbering like a dog in heat," said Izak Van Helsing, snapping his fingers. "Have you ever seen anything more pathetic?"

"...Or werewolves..."

"And what about the fish-men of..."

"Enough!" shouted the Sea Serpent, causing the ship to almost capsize. "I'll grant you that not all of our races are truly beautiful..."

"Or learned," said Izak Van Helsing. "You should have tried talking to the Last Ghoul of Lemuria. He could barely spell his name in Sanskrit."

"...Or learned," grudgingly admitted the Serpent, gritting his teeth, producing a noise not unlike the screech of chalk on a blackboard. "But we *are* ancient!" he finished in a triumphant tone.

"Yes, you are that. Can't argue about that, can we, darling?" said Izak Van Helsing to Scarlet Lips.

"Nope. Some of these monsters are really really old," she replied. "In fact, I've heard—but no, it would hardly be impolite to mention this before our towering scaly guest here."

"What have you heard, female?" roared the Serpent. "And be careful. I have a mind to end this most annoying of conversations right now and consign you all to Davy Jones' locker."

"But then, you wouldn't find out what she knows," pointed Izak Van Helsing.

"If you insist..." said Scarlet Lips.

"I do, I do," said the Serpent.

"Well, it's been said that some of you elder creatures are so old that... that... well, you know..."

"No, I don't," said the Serpent.

Scarlet Lips tapped her forehead slightly in an unmistakable gesture.

"...That you've all gone a little ga-ga," she finished.

"Ga-ga?" roared the Sea Serpent, causing a tear in the mizzen sail.

"Senile. Doddering. Feeble-minded."

"I know what 'ga-ga' means, female! I mastered your inane language 300 years ago!"

"Sorry," said Scarlet Lips, looking properly apologetic.

"She's right, you know," interjected Izak Van Helsing. "I've even heard some no doubt misguided souls claim that you can't even remember your own name."

"Of all the stupid things!... That's absurd! I am Jörmungandr, also known by the secret name of Uroborus and..."

Suddenly, there was a long silence. The Sea Serpent had realized that it had said too much, for his name was his secret, his secret was his name, and there was much power in both.

Izak Van Helsing smiled. It was an ugly, triumphant smile, nothing like the smile with which he had first greeted the Serpent.

From his pocket, he produced a bottle made of a substance that might have been glass, except that it was totally dark and did not reflect light.

It was a matter of mere seconds to incorporate the true name of the Sea Serpent into the eight conjurations of the Saaamaaa Ritual, recite them aloud, and thus force the creature inside the bottle.

"So much for the Sea Serpent," said Izak Van Helsing to Scarlet Lips. "He was much easier than I thought. They may be ancient and learned, but they sure are stupid. What's next on the list?"

"Something about a giant white whale, I think..."

Sacred Monster

December 13, 1968. A Friday.

Inside the empty hangar was a cross. It was made of wood, ancient wood, and it had been lovingly erected by the two monks.

On that cross was the Monster.

He was whimpering softly and occasionally tried to shake himself free, but the blood-encrusted leather bonds with which the monks had tied him to the cross would neither break nor slip. Besides, he had been drugged.

Two men entered.

"This is the Monster," said Father Rodin. "You know what to do."

"Yes," said Ohisver Van Helsing. "Damn you, yes, I do."

The Jesuit ignored his companion's angry outburst. From a leather pouch he carried over his shoulder, he pulled a dagger that was made of a spear's head mounted on a bronze handle. He offered it to his companion.

"This is Longinus' weapon. Go!"

Ohisver took the knife and walked slowly towards the cross. Towards the Monster.

The two monks silently stepped aside to let him pass.

"I'm sorry, I'm really sorry" said Van Helsing softly to the Monster. Then, with all his strength, he plunged the blade deep into the creature's chest.

The Monster screamed.

The Day Before...

When Ohisver Van Helsing returned from Tokyo, Zaka told him that he had a visitor waiting for him—a man who had simply introduced himself as "Father Rodin."

"So, you've come to collect, priest," said Ohisver to the Jesuit, coming straight to the point, without any words of welcome.

Father Rodin was a tall, almost ascetic man, with steel-grey hair. He was dressed in an ordinary black clergyman's suit. His face was that of an Inquisitor and in his eyes burned a fanatical flame. This was a man used to power, used to command, who brooked no disagreements.

"Yes, I have, Mr. Van Helsing," he replied. "A life for a life, a soul for a soul. It is the Eternal Covenant, isn't it?"

Ohisver poured himself a stiff drink from the liquor cabinet and drank it quickly. He did not bother to offer one to Rodin, for he knew the Jesuit didn't drink.

"Yes," he said. "I will honor our agreement. What do you want me to do?"

"I'll tell you in a moment," said the Jesuit. "You may find some comfort in knowing that you will perform a great deed in the service of our Holy Mother the Church."

"I care little for the Church."

"You will see the error of your ways in time, I'm sure. The Church has been generous towards your family over the centuries."

"Old stories. What do you want from me today?"

"Why, I want you to slay a Monster, of course," said Rodin with a mirthless smile.

"I don't understand."

Now, it was suddenly Father Rodin's turn to hesitate. Ohisver Van Helsing noticed that, for the time, the Jesuit avoided his eyes. The priest licked his thin lips then said:

"Throughout history, God has occasionally chosen to incarnate a portion of Himself into human form, a man whom we call His Son..."

"You mean, Jesus."

"Yes, Jesus—and perhaps a few others, whom we have failed to identify and destroy in time."

"Destroy the Son of God?" said Ohisver Van Helsing, surprised. "But isn't that against your faith?" Now he understood the Jesuit's reluctance to speak.

Father Rodin's nostrils flared. Van Helsing had never seen him this upset.

"We already have a Messiah. We already have a Church, Mr. Van Helsing," said the Jesuit, curtly. "We don't need any more."

"So you want me to slay the Son of God who apparently has returned. I get it. You don't want the competition."

"No!" shouted Rodin. Then, the priest composed himself. Calmly, he continued: "No, it's not just that. Think of the millions who have died during the crusades, all the *jihads*... Do we want God's word to be misinterpreted again, to start new faiths, to launch new armies of fanatics who will soon be wading in blood through our cities?"

"I see your point, I suppose. It's an interesting philosophical debate, anyway. I always wondered what your Church would do if Jesus were to come back. Now, I know. But you haven't really answered my original question. Why can't you do the job yourself? God knows you've slain your hundreds over the years, Rodin. Why choose *me* to be your executioner?"

"Because you slay monsters and the man we seek *is* a monster. A profanation of the Divine incarnated as mortal flesh; what could be more monstrous? He is what our French brethren call a *Monstre Sacré*, a Sacred Monster..."

"Still, you wouldn't invoke the pact we made 16 years ago in Brazil when you saved Maria's life..."

"Her soul."

"Yes, Maria's *soul*, if you only needed my expertise as a Van Helsing. Tell me the truth."

"It is a matter of doctrine..." Rodin began.

"Cut to the chase," said Ohisver Van Helsing.

"Very well. Our, er, spiritual investigations have led some of us to believe that the man who slays the Sacred Monster himself becomes cursed, loses his soul and, even after death, will not find eternal peace."

"Ha! Now the truth comes out. You're too chicken to do the job yourself and lose your precious immortality, so you want me to do it."

"A soul for a soul. You owe us."

"Very well, I'll do your dirty job, Rodin. It isn't everyday that one kills the Son of God, after all. And you can take your curse and stuff it, too. I'm a Van Helsing. We *are* the curse!"

Back to scene...

...The Monster screamed.

Then his body appeared to undergo a mysterious transformation. Before, he had seemed almost angelic, radiating a unique power, a divine charisma.

Now, he was just a man, a worn-out, tired-looking man—and yet, he lived—and yet, he breathed. The two monks carefully undid the straps, bandaged his wound, which, oddly, had stopped bleeding, and helped him back to his feet.

Ohisver Van Helsing, still clutching the bloodied dagger, turned towards Father Rodin.

"I don't understand. Didn't I just kill him?" he asked.

"Yes, you killed the Divine Essence that resided within him, but the Mortal Host lives on. Now he's just a poor, wretched, soulless man, doomed to die."

The Jesuit took the blade of Longinus from Ohisver Van Helsing's hand without a protest.

"We have refined our methods over the ages," the priest added. "Our spells no longer kill the mortal half of the Monster."

"So I am not...?"

"Oh, yes, I'm sorry to say, you are still most definitely damned. You *have* just killed His Son after all."

Outside, the monks helped the man into a cab. Las Vegas sparkled in the distance, like a Christmas tree incongruously deposited in the middle of the Nevada desert.

"You will remember nothing, Mr. Presley," said one of the monks, completing the spell of amnesia.

"Just... call me... Elvis," said the Man Who No Longer Was A Monster, slurring his words.

He needed a drink.

Don't Throw Granny to the Xhlingniarph

to Richard Bessière

"Why don't you use something from your vault as extra protection?" asked Zigor Side.

The attorney and his client, Hugo Van Helsing, were having breakfast at the Amsterdammer Club. In a couple of hours, they were scheduled to meet at the Central Park Boathouse with Prescott Brown of the Clock Company and a representative from Morrison, Morrison & Dodd.[6]

"What vault?" said Hugo.

Zigor burst out in a joyless laugh.

"Come on, Professor! This could just about be the most important meeting of your life—the most dangerous too, maybe. I'm doing my lawyerly duty here by suggesting that you improve your chances of getting out of it alive by having some kind of hidden ace up your sleeve, and you start going coy on me?"

"I don't know what you're talking about, Mr. Side," said Hugo, coldly.

"You're a terrible liar, you know."

Hugo was unable to repress a tight smile. "Not true. I'm an excellent liar," he said.

---

[6] This scene takes place during the events of Xavier Maumèjean's novel, *Freakshow!*, in 2008.

"For your common variety cop or immigration officer, maybe, but I'm a master of the bar. I've cross-examined some of the best liars in the world. You wouldn't stand ten minutes if I had you on the stand."

Hugo quickly finished his cup of tea, folded his napkin and then looked at his watch. "Very well, we still have some time left before we have to go. What do you want to know?" he asked.

"I've heard that you have a secret vault somewhere down here where you keep all kinds of dangerous artifacts and magical weapons, not unlike..."

Zigor lightly tapped the spot under his stained shirt where Hugo knew the Medallion of Damballah hung.

"That's true. We do have such a vault, but it would be sheer lunacy to try using any of the items we keep down there against our enemies. The catastrophes we might accidentally unleash would far exceed our current problems with Mr. Barnum."

"Well, yeah, but..."

"No ifs ands or buts, Counselor. Let me tell you the story of our last acquisition. In fact, I'll have our latest contributor tell it to you himself..."

Hugo Van Helsing got up and walked to a nearby table. There, he tapped on the shoulder of a middle-aged man with a mop of unruly brown hair and twinkling, blue eyes. After a few minutes of conversation, the man followed Hugo back to the table.

"Mr. Side, this is Sydney Gordon, features editor at *The New Sun*. Mr. Gordon, this is my attorney, Mr. Zigor Side."

Zigor had made a face when he had heard the name of the paper, something that did not escape the journalist.

"I know, I know," said Gordon, "we're a tad less reputable than the *Weekly World News*. My last headline was *Angelina Adopts Alien Baby*—and I'm proud of it. But I know you too, Counselor. You're hardly one to criticize when it comes to trawling the gutters."

"Mr. Gordon's paper and I have enjoyed a profitable and mutually-rewarding relationship over the years," interjected Hugo Van Helsing. "They have often generated information that proved crucial to us..."

"...And we, in turn, have enjoyed some of the world's juiciest exclusives. By the way, thanks for the Big B's phone number, Prof. He'll be our next featured celebrity."

"Mr. Gordon, I would like you to tell Mr. Side the story of the Xhlingniarph, in your own words. I want to convince him that whatever we bury in our vault is better left buried."

"My pleasure, Professor..." began Sydney Gordon.

Sydney Gordon's story:

They say that bad things always come in threes. I'm the living proof of that.

The first bad thing that happened to me, last Christmas, was Margaret's news that her mother Iris was coming to spend the holidays with us.

"Us" means the Gordon family, i.e.: Sydney, head of the household, at least according to the US census bureau form, Margaret, my wife, and Bud, my 20-year-old son. I'll be candid: at this point in my wretched life, I only have two dreams left. One is to see the Red Sox beat the Yankees, the other is to see Bud leave his computer and the lair that he calls his room to rejoin the human race.

So the news of Iris coming to spend the holidays with us definitely meant that I wouldn't be able to watch sports on TV and guaranteed Bud's isolation. So much for dreams.

Because, compared to Iris, Cruella deVil and the Wicked Witch of the West are like Mother Teresa, and I know what I'm talking about because I've met the Wicked Witch. Iris has buried five husbands, who probably preferred an earlier run towards their little plot of Heaven, as opposed to the continued existence in this Valley of Tears that their lives must have been like.

The second bad thing that happened—but that, I understood only later—was a letter that I received from an El Paso, Texas, attorney informing me that, during the sale of the old Gordon ancestral home, a.k.a. the shack, they had found a chest that belonged to my grandfather, the explorer Francis X. Gordon. The worthy shyster asked me if I wanted to take possession of it, which I could, as long as I paid him a hefty fee naturally, lawyers not being philanthropists. I'm a sentimental person, so I said yes. A bad mistake, as you will soon discover.

The third bad thing.... But let's not get ahead of ourselves...

On Christmas Eve, after the excellent meal cooked by Margaret, we gathered around the tree to open the presents. As we do every year, we had invited our friends, Professor Archibald Brent and his wife Gloria, to spend the evening with us. The word "presents" had even managed to convince Bud to crawl out of his lair. That boy had smelled the possibility of a new game for his PlayStation the way a starving ogre smells a virgin; his every instinct had told him that "Granny" hadn't come empty handed.

Let's talk about "Granny" for a moment. During the day, Iris had beaten her own world record in the Perfidious Statements contest, with new ground-breaking entries like: "Margaret, didn't you date a Lenny Goldberg in college? I've heard he was just appointed Ambassador to Filikistan." Or my favorite: "You know, they have pills for that sort of dysfunction nowadays," accompanied with a pointed look in my direction.

Bud's instincts had not led him astray. Granny had indeed brought with her the latest PlayStation game, *Killer Bondage Nuns IV*, and my son, who was smarter than he looked, and to my great surprise, pulled out a present wrapped in some tacky gift paper, to give to his grandmother.

"Oooh that's so sweet," cooed the Granny Monster. "This boy must take after his mother."

Once unwrapped, we discovered a small glass jar, Persian-style, with lovely painted swirls and characters on it, quite exquisite really, not at all the type of artsy present I would have expected Bud to buy. In fact, how had he bought it? If he had ordered it on line, we would have seen the delivery man. It was a mystery.

"For you, Granny," said my hypocritical son, simultaneously grabbing his videogame, then beating a quick retreat to his lair, just like an Ogre who has just received a copy of *3000 Ways to Serve Virgins* from the Good Cook Book Club of the Month and is eager to try a recipe.

If you watch CNN, you already know what happened next. Iris had the bright idea of removing the glass stopper that kept the jar closed. Immediately, a *Xhlingniarph* came out, the size of which made King Kong look like a Hobbit. The creature then began roaming through the city, devouring two US Army divisions, 12 fighter jets, 24 TV news vans, 3245 persons of good will, including seven Santa Claus and two Frenchmen.

I could write a book about it, but I already sold the film rights to Ryan Entertainment, so now I don't have to and you'll have to wait for the film. I'm that smart.

Archie eventually managed to decipher the characters painted on the jar. It was some kind of ancient tongue used by a long-gone tribe from Northern Afghanistan. It explained that the jar contained the spirit of the *Xhlingniarph* (that's what it sounded like), the God of Mean, bottled up by a Holy Man whose name has been forgotten by History—that bitch!

It then came out that Bud, pressed to find some kind of present for Iris, had broken into Francis X. Gordon's chest, which I had stored in the attic. A fractured lock, some wrapping paper and presto—instant gift!

So I hear you ask, the third bad thing happened when Iris uncorked the jar and freed the Xhlingniarph?

Not at all! We New Yorkers are used to giant monsters walking down Fifth Avenue, swallowing tourists like M&Ms. No big deal.

The third bad thing actually happened when Iris said: "This is all your fault, Sydney. If you gave that boy enough money, he wouldn't have to ransack through your old garbage to find a suitable Christmas present for his dear old Granny."

At that point, I don't know what came over me, but I pushed Iris back and she fell into the jar.

Yes, you heard me right. *Into* the jar. *Inside* it.

And right there and then, the Xhlingniarph vanished. Poof! In one fell swoop. Just like that. Everyone and everything he had swallowed before found themselves back exactly where they were when the demon had grabbed them, with not even a slight headache.

Archie explained that the Xhlingniarph required a sacrifice, the gift of someone incredibly mean and nasty. Where 3425 New Yorkers had not sufficed, Iris, on the other hand, had done the job.

So I hear you say: "All's well that ends well, right?" For New York, undoubtedly. But for me, not so much. If I don't want to continue sleeping on the living room couch where Margaret has exiled me, I'd better pray that Archie finds a way to extract Iris from the jar.

And that's the third bad thing.

ABOUT THE COVER

Zombie Harbors are havens of peace where zombies who have managed to escape from human persecution can find refuge and organize a resistance. In the universe of *Zombie Harbor*, the living dead have been enslaved by the humans, who use them as laborers for the dangerous and/or degrading jobs that were once performed by the poor.

Zombie Harbor is a shared fictional universe created by Hardtone and Yoz, focusing on the theme of the zombies and the development and exploration of a complex universe in various media such as comic books, photonovels, short features, games, etc.

The first step in that development process was the launching of a website, www.zombieharbor.com, which serves a link between our world and that of *Zombie Harbor* by fostering the creation of a community of "online zombies" and enable our members to share their artistic creations.

Four months after its launch in late 2007, the *Zombie Harbor* site has gathered more than 10,000 visitors, features half-a-dozen galleries (including the photo of Krystal Tombale, used for the cover of this book), counts 78 zombie members and more than 40 regular creators and contributors.

Our next step is the creation of anthology comic book, *Zombie Harbor Tales*.

Hardtone

Printed in the United Kingdom
by Lightning Source UK Ltd.
129274UK00001B/127-129/P